Echoes of the Rain

R. RIVERA

ISBN: 9798218623104 (Paperback)

Library of Congress Control Number: 2025903773

Printed in the United States of America

This is for all the aspiring writers who think they can't make it. If I can do it, I know you can. Sometimes, we need a little kick to get us motivated. Well, here's your kick. Here's your motivation. You've got this!

"Guilt is the ghost we carry, unseen but never absent. It lingers in the quiet spaces, the rain-soaked roads, and the reflection of eyes we can no longer meet."

Unknown

Preface

Some stories never leave you. They sit in the back of your mind, whispering and waiting for the right moment to be heard. Echoes of the Rain, originally titled The Accident, is one of these stories.

I started writing this almost a decade ago. Sometimes I would pour myself into it, only to step away for years, unsure if I would ever return. It haunted me, not just the story itself, but the feeling that it needed to be finished. It became a cycle: writing, pausing, doubting. Then trying agian.

But this time, I refused to let it go unfinished. This time, I made myself see it through to the end.

And now, here you are, holding the completed work, the story that once felt like a ghost in my mind, now brought to life of these pages. I hope you enjoy it.

I hope it lingers with you, the way it lingered with me.

R. Rivera

Contents

Prologue

B ecky's love for storms was written in the very first moments of her life. She was born on a night when the sky cracked open, rain pouring in thick sheets, lightning splitting the darkness with each violent flash. The hospital's power failed just minutes before her arrival, plunging the delivery room into shadow save for the eerie glow of emergency lights. The doctors worked under the hum of the generator, their voices steady but tense as the storm rattled the windows and shook the building's foundation.

Her mother would later tell her that, in the instant she let out her first cry, a bolt of lightning struck just outside the hospital, illuminating the room as if the sky itself was welcoming her.

"It was like the storm knew you were here," her mother whispered years later, brushing a hand through Becky's curls as thunder rolled in the distance. "Like it was part of you from the very beginning."

Even as a baby, Becky had been soothed storms. While other infants wailed at thunder, she would drift to sleep to the steady drum of rain against the roof. AS she grew, she spent hours on the porch, legs tucked beneath her as she watched downpours transform the world. She never saw storms as danger they we alive, electric, beautiful. And they had always been with her.

Now, at twenty-seven, that pull had never faded.

The café hummed with quiet conversation and the hiss of the espresso machine, cinnamon and coffee thick in the air. Outside, autumn's restless wind sent golden leaves dancing across the pavement. The sky had shifted from a crisp blue to a muted gray, clouds knitting together in a slow, ominous crawl.

Becky stirred her cappuccino, her gaze drifting toward the window. Each gust rattled the glass, sending a thrill prickling beneath her skin.

Across from her, Aaron scrolled through his phone, his brow furrowing before he muttered, "Uh-oh."

Becky's attention snapped back. "Uh-oh? What kind of 'uh-oh'?"

He turned the screen toward her. A swirling mass of blue and green loomed over their town on the radar, the colors shifting as they closed in. A bold red banner stretched across the top:

Severe Storm Warning: Possible Flooding & High Winds Expected.

Her pulse quickened. She set her cup down with a grin. "Finally. A real storm."

Aaron shook his head, exhaling. "Of course you'd be thrilled."

"You know I love storms. They make everything feel... alive." Her fingers tapped the table as if echoing distant thunder.

Aaron leaned back, arms crossed. "Most people see that warning and think about supplies. You see it and start hoping for lightning to put on a show."

Becky smirked. "What's the point of a storm if it doesn't make you feel something?"

He studied her, amused but concerned. She had always been this way—drawn to the wild, to the unpredictable. And it worried him.

"Just promise me one thing," Aaron said finally.

Becky arched a brow. "Depends."

"No running outside like a maniac when it hits." His tone was firm, but his eyes softened.

Becky laughed, the sound light against the weight of the storm outside. "I'll try to contain myself."

"That's not a promise," he warned.

She only winked. "That's because you know I don't make promises I can't keep."

Aaron groaned, but there was no real frustration. This was Becky. She would always be drawn to the storm, no matter how unpredictable or dangerous it might be.

A sudden howl of wind rattled the café windows, sending leaves skittering against the glass. Becky's gaze lingered on the shifting gray sky, anticipation rising like a tide.

Later that night, the storm arrived in full force. Rain slashed the windows of her home, lightning carving jagged streaks across the sky. Becky stood at her window, unable to look away. The storm had always been her comfort, her constant companion.

But tonight, as thunder shook the walls and the wind howled through the trees, something felt... different.

A flash of lightning illuminated the yard. For a split second, she saw it—

a figure standing at the tree line.

Her breath caught. The next flash revealed nothing but empty space. A trick of the light, surely.

And yet, she could not shake the feeling that something—or someone—was out there.

Watching.

Waiting.

CHAPTER ONE

A Storm Without End

T he rain hadn't let up all night. It poured relentlessly, drumming against the roof in a steady rhythm that filled the house, drowning out all other sound. The wind howled against the siding, rattling the windows in their frames as if demanding to be let in. Distant thunder grumbled low across the sky, a slow, rolling growl that never quite faded before another rumble took its place. The storm was relentless, an unbroken force pressing against the house, and yet Becky found herself comforted by its presence. The storm outside mirrored the one inside her head.

At her desk, Becky sat hunched over her laptop, fingers hovering over the keyboard. The pale glow illuminated the scattered notes, the half-empty cup of coffee, and the bowl of fresh berries beside her. Their sweetness mixed with the bitter remnants of caffeine, an odd but familiar contrast. Her dark brown hair, hastily tucked behind her ears, had come loose in places, framing her freckled face. She frowned at the screen, dissatisfaction settling deep.

She had been working for hours, trying to finish an article before her looming deadline. The words still felt hollow, lacking the precision she was known for. Freelance writing granted her independence, but deadlines had a way of creeping up, relentless as the storm outside. This one, in particular, had been weighing on her all week, and she couldn't afford to fall behind.

More than that, she didn't want to. This article was more than just another assignment; it was an opportunity, one that had landed in her lap almost unexpectedly. A well-known publication had reached out to her, impressed by one of her previous pieces. If she delivered something exceptional, there was a real chance this could turn into steady work, the kind that could finally give her a break from the constant hustle of freelancing. The kind that meant security.

But what if she failed?

That thought had been creeping in all night, whispering just behind every half-formed sentence. What if this was her shot and she ruined it? What if she turned in something mediocre and the opportunity slipped away before she even had a chance to grasp it?

Her fingers drummed against the desk. She reread the last paragraph for the fifth time, her mind struggling to grasp what was missing. She hated this part—when the words blurred together, when inspiration ran dry, when the pressure of time made every sentence feel forced. She needed this article to be good. No, not just good—great. Something that proved she was still sharp, still capable of delivering work worth reading. Worth publishing.

She leaned back in her chair, rubbing her temples. Outside, lightning slashed across the sky, momentarily revealing skeletal branches twisting in the wind. The sight sent a familiar thrill through her. She had always loved storms—their raw energy, their unpredictability. They made the world feel alive.

That had been part of why she started writing in the first place. The ability to capture a feeling, a moment, to give life to something that existed only in words—that was what had drawn her in. But now? Now it felt different. Writing had become a necessity, a means to survive rather than an outlet of passion. She still loved it, but somewhere along the way, the joy of it had started to dull under the weight of expectations, of deadlines, of the constant need to prove herself.

Another gust of wind slammed against the house, rattling the windows harder this time. Becky exhaled sharply, rubbing the exhaustion from her eyes. Maybe a break would help. Just five minutes. Maybe ten. Long enough to clear her head before trying again.

She grabbed the bowl of berries and padded toward her dresser, stripping off her day-old clothes in favor of sweatpants and a loose hoodie. The fabric was soft and comforting. It felt good to be out of the stiff jeans she had thrown on that morning with the hopeful intention of feeling more put-together.

As she moved through the room, she caught her reflection in the mirror. Tired eyes. Slightly sunken cheeks. Lips pressed into a tight, thin line. She looked as exhausted as she felt. It was not just physical fatigue. It was something deeper, something that had been building for a while now.

Shaking her head, she turned away and climbed into bed, setting the bowl beside her on the mattress. Maybe she should just finish the article in the morning. No. She didn't have that luxury.

She pulled the blanket over herself, sinking into the warmth. The rain continued its steady drum against the house, the wind still howling in protest. Becky closed her eyes for a moment, listening, feeling. The storm was not going anywhere. Neither was she.

Then, somewhere in the distance, a sound carried on the wind.

A whisper.

Or maybe... nothing at all.

The thought flickered and vanished, swallowed by the storm.

Her breathing slowed. Exhaustion took hold.

For now, the storm was just a storm.

But tomorrow, everything would change.

Restless Thoughts

She shifted the bowl of berries to the side and propped herself up on her elbows, her gaze fixed on the window. There was something hypnotic about how the rain streaked down the glass in winding trails, each droplet racing the next to the bottom of the pane. It was chaos in motion, the kind of chaos that demanded attention and made her pulse quicken just a little.

Becky set her phone down, the glow disappearing as the screen went dark, leaving her room lit only by the faint golden glow of her bedside lamp. The storm's noise filled the space, drowning out the world beyond the walls of her home. She could hear every creak of the house as the wind buffeted it, every gust pushing against the sturdy walls with a ferocity that made her grateful for their strength.

She stared out the window, mesmerized by the storm. Watching something so destructive and uncontrollable was a strange kind of peace. It reminded her of how small she was in the grand scheme of things, how insignificant her worries seemed compared to the power of nature.

She leaned back against her pillow, her fingers drumming idly against the edge of the bowl. She thought about the errands she needed to run tomorrow, the laundry piling up in the basket by her closet, and the dwindling contents of her fridge. The thought of leaving the house in weather like this made her groan softly. She hated errands. They felt like such a waste of time—little tasks piling up until they became a mountain she couldn't avoid.

But the storm would not last forever, and the world would return to normal. It always did.

The Storm Fades into Sleep

The clock on her nightstand blinked 11:47 PM in soft red digits. Becky sighed, letting her head sink into the pillow. The rain pounded ceaselessly against the roof, its rhythmic drumming resonating deep within her as if the storm had found a way to inhabit her body. The wind roared again, shaking the windowpane with a force that might have started someone else, but Becky remained still. She closed her eyes, surrendering to the raw energy outside.

The Storm was wild, untamed—a cacophony of fury—yet, within its destructive power, she felt an inexplicable calm, a strange solace that she couldn't fully understand.

Her breathing slowed, and her mind wandered. The flashes of lightning and the rolling thunder became a kind of rhythm, a lullaby that pulled her deeper into the edges of sleep.

Then—CRACK!

A sharp, deafening snap tore through the air, so sudden that Becky's eyes flew open. The sound was different from the rolling thunder. Sharper. Closer.

Her heart pounded as she pushed herself up onto her elbows, listening intently. The wind had howled all night but this... this had been something else. Something breaking.

Her gaze flickered toward the window, and for a moment, she thought of the neighbor's tree—the ancient oak that had stood through decades of storms. Had it finally fallen?

Another gust of wind sent sheets of rain pounding against the glass. Becky held her breath, half-expecting to hear another impact, but the storm swallowed everything. The house settled again, creaking under the strain of the wind.

She exhaled, shaking her head. Maybe it had been a trash can knocked over, or a branch from another tree snapping in the wind. She wanted to check, to see if the oak was still standing, but exhaustion pressed down on her now, heavier than before.

Her head sank back into the pillow. The storm raged on, its steady drumming against the roof, a constant reminder that she was safe, tucked away inside.

for a fleeting moment, just before the darkness took her, Becky thought she heard something beneath the storm's noise—a faint sound, like a voice carried on the wind.

But the thought drifted away as quickly as it had come, lost in the unrelenting rain.

CHAPTER TWO

The Morning After

Morning arrived with an eerie stillness.

Becky stirred before her alarm went off, caught in the foggy space between dreams and waking. Images flickered behind her eyes—flashes of lightning, the roar of wind, a voice lost in the rain. The details slopped away as the shrill beep of her alarm shattered the quiet. She jolted upright with a sharp inhale, her heart pounding before she remembered where she was.

The storm. The weight of it still clung to her like a phantom pressing against her chest. She had slept—she could feel in the stiffness of her limbs, the dull ache in her shoulders from lying in one position too long—but it hadn't been restful.

She groaned, flailing her arm out blindly until her hand found the clock and silenced it with a resounding smack. For a moment, she just laid there, staring at the ceiling. The rain had lessened to a faint drizzle, a far cry from the chaos of the night before, but still enough to keep the world drenched in gray.

Forcing herself to move, she swung her legs over the edge of the bed and winced as her bare feet met the cold floor. The room was dim, weak morning light filtering through the thick clouds outside. The house felt unnaturally quiet now that the storm had passed, the absence of its relentless pounding almost unsettling.

Dragging herself to the kitchen, she moved with the sluggish heaviness of lingering exhaustion. The faint aroma of coffee filled the air, already brewing in her machine—an automatic setting she had programed ages ago. She reached for a mug, her movements slow and mechanical, like her body hadn't quite caught up to the fact that she was awake. The warmth of the ceramic felt soothing in her hand as she poured herself a cup, but when she took a sip, she winced.

Too hot.

She set it down and leaned against the counter, rubbing at her temper as her eyes drifted toward the window.

The street outside was a mess. Fallen branches littered the pavement, tangled piles of leaves clogged the storm drains, and trash cans laid on their sides, contents scattered across the sidewalk. Pools of water shimmered on the asphalt, reflecting the pale morning sky.

And then her eyes landed on the oak tree.

It was still standing.

Becky narrowed her gaze, half-expecting to see it cracked in half or at least missing limbs. But, aside from a few smaller branches snapped near the top, it had survived. She exhaled, half-impressed, half-bewildered. After last night's winds, she had been almost certain she'd wake up to an empty patch of earth where it once stood.

Shaking her head, she grab her coffee again, this time taking it slower, more cautious sip. It was bitter—she hadn't added sugar yet—but its warmth cut through the morning chill. She shuffled over to the living room and turned on the TV, letting the soft glow and murmur of voices fill the space.

The local news greeted her, the anchor's voice cheerful in an almost inappropriate way, given the grim footage flashing on the screen.

"Last night's storm caused significant damage across the county," the woman reported, her tone upbeat despite the words. "We've received reports of downed power lines, uprooted trees, and widespread flooding. Authorities are urging residents to use caution as crews work to clear the debris."

Becky's eyes wandered to the images on the screen. A crushed car beneath the weight of a fallen tree. Broken windows in homes, now exposed to the elements. A residential street swallowed by murky floodwaters.

She sighed and turned the TV off. She could watch only so much destruction before it started to feel suffocating.

After rinsing out her mug, she headed for the bathroom, hoping a shower would shake of the unease still clinging to her. The water hit the tile in a steady, rhythmic cascade, drowning out the lingering silence of the house. She let the heat loosen the tension in her muscles, but even as it washed over her, the heavy feeling in her chest refused to fade.

It was not fear-not exactly.

It was something heavier, something deeper, something she couldn't quite name.

The storm had passed, but it felt like it had left something behind.

The Sky Hears Her

The storm's over, she told herself. It's just leftover drizzle.

But as soon as she slid into the driver's seat and turned the ignition, the sky seemed to hear her thoughts—because the moment her hands gripped the wheel, the rain started up again.

Not a soft drizzle.

A heavy, rolling downpour.

The kind that swallowed sound, blurred vision, and turned the world into nothing but a smear of water and shifting darkness.

Becky swallowed hard, glancing at the sky through her windshield. The timing was eerie.

She shook off the unease, exhaling as she turned on her wipers. It was just rain. The storm hadn't really ended—it had only paused.

She tightened her grip on the wheel and pulled onto the wet road, determined to get through her errands before the next wave of the storm truly began.

She had no idea it had already started.

Through the Rain

Becky pulled out of her driveway, the wipers moving in steady, rhythmic swipes against the rain-slicked windshield. The sky was a brooding gray, thick with low-hanging clouds that stretched across the horizon like a storm still considering its next move. Puddles had collected along the sidewalks, distorting neon signs and traffic lights into shimmering, fractured reflections.

The roads weren't empty, but there was a hush to the town, a dampened quiet in the spaces between passing cars. She drove cautiously, the pavement still wet from the earlier downpour, her tires sending up tiny sprays of water as she moved through the streets.

Her first stop was the grocery store, a small local chain with flickering fluorescent lights above its entrance. The automatic doors hissed open as she approached, and the sudden blast of artificial warmth and citrus-scented cleaner was almost jarring after the damp chill outside.

Inside, the store was oddly quiet, a few scattered customers moving between the aisles. The usual hum of casual conversations was subdued, as if people were still shaking off the weight of the storm.

Becky grabbed a basket and moved slowly through the aisles, selecting the basics—milk, eggs, coffee. Then, almost as an afterthought, she added a pint of salted caramel ice cream.

As she reached the checkout, an older woman with silver-streaked hair scanned her items with unhurried precision. She glanced at Becky's damp jacket.

"Did the storm hit your area badly?"

Becky shook her head. "It was intense, but not too bad. I loved every minute of it."

The woman chuckled, shaking her head. "You sound like my grandson. He sits on the porch like he's waiting for the sky to open up and swallow him whole."

"Sounds like a smart kid," Becky said with a smirk, swiping her card.

The woman handed her the receipt, still smiling. "Storm's not done yet, you know. Might be worse by nightfall."

Becky only nodded, gathering her bags before stepping back into the damp air.

Her next stop was the movie rental shop, one of the few relics of the past still standing in town. The glass door chimed as she stepped inside, and she was immediately greeted by the familiar scent of buttered popcorn and plastic DVD cases.

She traced a finger along the rows of movie titles, the fluorescent lights overhead casting a pale glow over the shelves.

"Anything good?" the teenage clerk behind the counter asked, chin propped in his hand.

"Hoping for something new," Becky mused. "Maybe a thriller. Something with a storm in it, if I'm lucky."

The kid smirked, shaking his head. "Figures. you are one of those storm people, huh?"

"Guilty as charged."

She settled on an old Hitchcock film—*The Birds*—not quite a storm, but close enough, then made her way out into the misty drizzle that had replaced the heavier downpour.

Next was the furniture store, a place she'd been meaning to visit for weeks. The shop smelled of varnished wood and fabric softener, the polished floors lined with neatly arranged displays of dining sets, bookshelves, and plush couches that begged to be tested.

A young saleswoman approached with a practiced smile. "Looking for anything in particular today?"

"Just browsing," Becky said, running her fingers over the armrest of a recliner.

"Well, let me know if you need help. we arehaving a sale on sectionals this week."

Becky nodded absently, already picturing how a new couch might fit into her living room, how it might feel to curl up on one of those deep cushions while rain lashed against the windows.

Maybe another time.

After a quick lunch at a café—just a turkey sandwich and a cup of black coffee—she wandered into a clothing boutique, halfheartedly flipping through racks of sweaters and jeans. She didn't need anything new, but there was something soothing about the routine, the mindless act of touching fabric, of watching the colors blur together under the shop's soft lighting.

By the time she stepped back outside, the sky had darkened again.

The steady drizzle had transformed into something heavier, more insistent. Streetlights flickered to life, their golden glow reflecting in the wet pavement.

She pulled her phone from her pocket and frowned at the missed call from Aaron.

Leaning against the side of her car, she called him back, shielding the screen from the rain.

"Hey," he answered on the first ring. "I was starting to think you got swept away."

"Not yet," Becky laughed, unlocking her car. "But I wouldn't have minded."

"I bet," he said. "Storm hit hard around your place?"

"It was intense but not bad. I loved every minute of it."

Aaron chuckled. "Of course you did. Just be careful, okay? You never know when it can get worse."

She rolled her eyes but smiled despite herself. "I think I'll survive."

"Just saying," he replied. "The way you talk about storms, I half expect you to walk straight into a hurricane one day just to see what happens."

She smirked. "That does not sound like the worst idea."

"Yeah, well, I'd like to keep my favorite storm-chasing weirdo in one piece, so do not push your luck."

There was a warmth in her chest at that, something grounding. "Noted. I'll call you later."

"Deal. Be safe."

She hung up, glancing at the time before tossing her phone onto the passenger seat. 6:45 PM.

As she turned onto the main road leading home, she noticed how much harder the rain had gotten, the steady hiss against her windshield intensifying. The storm was not over yet.

Maybe Aaron was right. Maybe she should be careful.

But as she drove through the rain-slicked streets, she felt it creeping in again—that quiet, electric anticipation curling in her veins.

She loved this.

She always had.

She had spent so much of her life chasing this feeling, lingering in storms when others sought shelter, soaking in the chaos while others avoided it. And tonight, the storm felt different.

Larger.

Heavier.

It pressed down on the world in a way she couldn't quite explain, as though something vast and unseen was shifting just beyond her line of sight.

The road ahead stretched out in a ribbon of wet asphalt, gleaming under the streetlights. She should have gone straight home.

Instead, she turned down a side street, one that wound toward the lake just beyond town. The storm had darkened the water into an endless, restless void, raindrops vanishing into its surface like ink bleeding into fabric.

She pulled over at a small clearing and shut off the engine, watching as the storm danced across the water. The wind sent ripples moving in uneven patterns, trees bending under its force. The sky was alive with movement—not just clouds, but something deeper, something unseen threading through the storm's restless heart.

She didn't know how long she sat there, just watching.

But as lightning cracked across the sky, illuminating the lake in a burst of cold white light, she realized something:

Tonight didn't feel like just another storm.

It felt like a warning.

CHAPTER THREE

A Sudden Interruption

The rain was endless.

It poured from the sky in thick sheets, hammering Becky's windshield with relentless force. The wipers fought to keep up, swiping back and forth in a frantic struggle against the downpour. But it was too much. The world outside blurred into distorted light, water, and darkness.

The rhythmic thudding of raindrops against the roof was deafening, drowning out even the soft hum of the engine as she navigated the slick, winding road.

She was not heading straight home.

After finishing her errands, she had taken the long way back, winding through familiar backroads that felt different under the storm's fury. Something about driving through heavy rain always gave her a strange sense of peace—like she was watching the world reset itself.

But tonight, it didn't feel like a reset.

It felt like a warning.

The trees lining the road loomed taller than usual, their skeletal branches whipping violently in the wind. The asphalt ahead gleamed under her headlights, an endless river of black reflecting the occasional flicker of lightning.

Becky gripped the wheel tighter, her fingers stiff and aching.

Get a grip, Becky.

It's just a storm. You love storms.

You've driven through worse.

Still, something about tonight felt... wrong.

The Dog and the Stranger

The road curved sharply ahead, and Becky instinctively eased off the gas. Her headlights swept across the bend, illuminating slick pavement and swirling mist.

Then—movement.

A flicker on the edge of her vision.

She leaned forward slightly, pulse quickening.

Something was there.

A shape darted onto the road.

Becky's breath caught.

A dog. A scruffy, drenched mutt, bolting into the street. Its fur was plastered to its thin frame, eyes wide with terror. She knew, in a gut-wrenching instant, she would not stop in time.

But something else was there, too.

Beyond the dog, a figure. Still. Watching. Waiting.

The moment stretched, endless.

Becky yanked the wheel.

Her foot hovered over the brake.

"Shit—"

The tires shrieked, slipping on the rain-slick asphalt. The car fishtailed, wrenched sideways as she fought for control.

And then.

Someone.

The man in the road.

Still standing. Still unmoving. Still waiting.

Her breath hitched. The headlights hit him full-on.

Wide eyes. Dark hoodie.

No reaction.

She barely had time to scream.

A sickening impact.

A flash of movement.

Then, there was nothing.

Her world tilted, spinning in a blur of rain and twisting shadows.

And then—

Silence.

A Terrible Realization

Becky's breath came in ragged, uneven gulps.

The car had stopped—somehow. The acrid scent of burnt rubber mixed with the metallic tang of rain. The wipers screeched, dragging streaks of something dark across the glass.

Her hands would not move.

Her pulse pounded.

What just happened?

A wave of nausea coiled in her stomach. This was not real. It couldn't be.

She forced herself to move, her fingers shaking as they fumbled for the door handle. The nausea surged as she pushed it open.

The storm swallowed her whole.

Rain hammered down, soaking through her clothes in seconds. Wind screamed through the trees, snatching at her hair and clawing at her skin.

She stepped forward.

Her boots splashed in the deepening puddles.

"Hello?"

The word barely carried over the storm.

No answer.

Her eyes darted through the shifting shadows.

She knew she had hit something. Someone.

But where—?

Then she saw it.

Just beyond the reach of her headlights, sprawled across the asphalt.

A shape.

A body.

Oh, God.

Her breath hitched. Her limbs felt leaden, every instinct screaming at her to stay back.

But she moved forward anyway.

The man lay crumpled, limbs twisted at angles that shouldn't be possible. His hoodie clung to his frame, soaked through. Rainwater pooled around him, dark and rippling.

Her hands flew to her mouth.

"Sir?"

A whisper. Barely a sound.

She inched closer, her heartbeat hammering against her ribs.

Something was wrong.

Very, very wrong.

Her gaze swept over him. The way he lay—off, unnatural, wrong in a way she couldn't yet name.

The slump of his shoulders.

The awkward bend of his neck.

The way his hoodie collapsed inward, as if—

No.

Her mind resisted, refused. Her eyes darted past the body, searching for an anchor, for something that made sense.

Then she saw it.

A shape in the mud. A pale curve, barely visible through the rain. It looked like—

No.

She took a step closer, and the truth crashed over her all at once.

It was not just the body that was wrong.

It was what was missing.

A few feet away, resting in the mud like a discarded mask—

His head.

Her breath hitched violently.

His eyes—open.

Green. Piercing. Fixed on her.

And worst of all—

He was smiling.

A strangled noise tore from her throat as she stumbled backward.

No.

No, no, no, no, no.

Her body trembled, her fingers fumbling inside her jacket pocket.

Her phone—where was her phone?

She yanked it out, clutching the cold metal like a lifeline.

Her fingers barely managed to dial before the screen blurred with raindrops.

She turned back toward the body, breath coming fast, uneven.

The smile was still there.

Frozen. Unmoving.

The wind howled through the trees, branches groaning, shifting.

Her pulse pounded against her ribs.

And then the thought came, cold and creeping—

Why was there no blood?

Her stomach lurched.

She squeezed her eyes shut. Dial. Dial. Dial.

The phone rang.

She turned away from the body, pressing it to her ear with trembling fingers.

Static.

A crackle on the line. The storm distorting the sound.

Then—

A voice.

Not the operator.

Not someone on the other end.

Something else.

A whisper.

From behind her.

The phone slipped from her fingers, vanishing into the mud.

She didn't turn around.

CHAPTER FOUR

The Call

Becky's hands trembled as she dropped to her knees, the cold rain soaking through her jeans in an instant. Her breath came in shallow gasps, misting in the air as she scrambled in the mud, fingers numb and slick with rain. Where was it?

Her phone. She had dropped it.

The ground was a swirling mess of puddles and sodden leaves, the thick scent of damp earth mingling with something sharper—metallic. Blood.

Her breath hitched, and then—there.

She spotted the faint glow of her phone's screen, half-buried in the muck. Her fingers closed around it, the casing slick and cold as she wiped it frantically against her jacket.

The screen flickered, distorted with streaks of water, but it still worked.

And that was when she saw it.

Her call log.

There was no received call. No missed call.

Nothing.

The breath in her throat turned to ice.

Had she imagined it?

That whisper—that voice. Had it even been real?

Becky squeezed her eyes shut, forcing herself to breathe. She couldn't lose it now. Not here. Not in the middle of the storm, not with a body lying just feet away.

Her hands shook violently as she tapped 9-1-1.

The dial tone barely had time to register before a voice clicked in, calm and professional.

"911, what's your emergency?"

Becky sucked in a sharp breath. Say something.

"I—I was in an accident," she stammered, her voice barely above a whisper. "I hit someone."

A slight pause. Then, measured, steady: "Okay, ma'am, I understand. Are you injured?"

Becky shook her head, though the dispatcher couldn't see her. "I do not think so. I hit my head on the airbag, but I'm not—" She swallowed hard. "It's not me. It's him."

"The person you hit?"

Becky's voice broke. "He's dead."

Another pause. The dispatcher's voice remained steady, but there was a careful hesitation now. "Alright, ma'am. I need you to stay calm. Can you tell me your location?"

Becky blinked, glancing around wildly as if the darkness would somehow give her an answer. The rain had blurred everything—the road signs, the distant tree line, even the turn she had taken just minutes before. Where the hell was she?

Then, she saw something that made her stomach lurch.

The hooded man's head was lying a few feet away, his lifeless eyes open. But his mouth... it was still moving.

It was whispering.

She closed her eyes and shook her head. This can't be real. She turned away from the body and opened her eyes.

"I—I do not know," she admitted, her voice rising. "I was driving home from Lakeshore—there was a dog in the road, and I swerved, and then he was just there. I hit him, and now he's—oh my God—he's—"

She gagged, turning away from the body.

The dispatcher's voice cut through her panic. "Ma'am, I need you to take a deep breath. Are there any landmarks nearby?"

Becky forced herself to look. Through the haze of rain, she spotted a wooden sign, half-covered in ivy near the tree line. Faded letters.

"Deer Hollow Road," she gasped. "Near the old Pineside Barn. Please. Send someone."

"Emergency responders are on the way, but I need you to stay on the line. Are there any other vehicles involved?"

"No. Just me. Just—"

Becky squeezed her eyes shut. The impact. The way his body had crumpled. The way he had looked at her.

The way he had smiled.

Her breath hitched again.

The dispatcher's voice hardened slightly. "Ma'am, can you safely approach the victim?"

Becky recoiled. Her skin crawled at the thought. "I—I don't think I can."

"I understand. But I need you to check if he's breathing."

No.

"He's not," she croaked.

"Ma'am, I need you to confirm."

A sharp tremor tore through Becky's body. The words slipped from her lips before she could stop them.

"He doesn't have a head!"

Silence.

The rain drummed against the pavement, filling the gap where words should have been.

The dispatcher's voice returned—careful now. "I'm sorry... you are saying the victim's head is... missing?"

Becky's throat closed. "It's—" A choked breath. "It's a few feet away. He's looking at me."

Another pause. This time, longer.

Then, the dispatcher spoke again, her voice still professional—but slower now, more deliberate. "Okay, ma'am. I need you to take a step back. Do not approach the body. Help is on the way."

Becky barely heard her. The world was closing in. Her vision tunneled, her skin clammy with cold sweat. She swayed on her feet, one hand gripping the car door for balance.

"He was smiling," she whispered.

"Ma'am?"

"When I hit him," Becky's voice was barely her own. "When he looked at me through the windshield before I—before I—"

She swallowed hard.

"He was smiling."

The dispatcher hesitated. "Are you certain, ma'am?"

A weak, hollow laugh escaped Becky's lips. "I do not know what I'm certain of anymore."

The sound of distant sirens cut through the storm, flashing red and blue flickering through the rain.

"Ma'am, officers are arriving now. Do you see them?"

Becky blinked at the approaching lights.

"Yes," she murmured. "I see them."

Her knees buckled.

The last thing she heard before the world tilted—

"you are safe now."

But as the darkness swallowed her, Becky was not sure she believed that.

Emergency Response & Police Investicagation

The world around Becky faded in and out, a murky blur of cold rain, flashing lights, and distant voices. The sharp scent of wet asphalt and burnt rubber mixed with something metallic—blood, her mind supplied numbly. She barely registered the sensation of her body collapsing, her knees hitting the damp ground before everything went dark.

"We've got a live one, she's coming to."

The voice was male, deep but not unkind. Becky's eyes fluttered open to see a face hovering above her, framed by the shifting glow of red and blue lights. Rain pattered against her skin, mixing with the sweat clinging to her brow. The world still felt unsteady, like she was trying to wake from a dream that refused to let her go.

"Hey, take it easy," the man said, his tone gentle but firm. His fingers pressed lightly against her wrist, checking her pulse. "You fainted. Can you hear me?"

Becky tried to nod, but the movement made her stomach lurch. She sucked in a breath, the cold air burning in her lungs.

Another voice chimed in—a woman's this time. "Ma'am, my name's Susan. I'm with EMS. Do you know where you are?"

Becky blinked sluggishly, her mind sluggishly grasping at the edges of reality. "The road," she rasped. "Deer Hollow..."

"Good," Susan said, her voice soothing. "Can you tell me your name?"

"...Becky."

"Alright, Becky, you took a bit of a fall there," Susan continued. "You hit your head when you went down, but your vitals look stable."

She lifted a penlight, flicking it across Becky's vision. "Follow the light for me."

Becky tried to comply, her pupils sluggishly tracking the movement. The paramedic's gaze flickered with subtle concern before she pulled the light away.

"How are you feeling?" Susan asked.

"Like I got hit by a truck," Becky murmured, her voice hoarse. Then, she let out a weak, humorless laugh. "Or... like I hit someone with one."

Susan's lips pressed together in a thin line. "Can you sit up for me? Slow and steady."

Becky let the paramedics guide her into an upright position, the rain still drizzling over them in a steady mist. The flashing lights cast eerie shadows on the pavement, illuminating the wreckage around her. The crumpled front of her car. The shattered windshield.

And beyond that...

Becky's stomach twisted violently. She tore her gaze away.

"Try to take slow breaths," Susan said, pressing a stethoscope to Becky's chest. "Your heart's racing."

"No kidding," Becky muttered, but her voice was barely above a whisper.

Susan exchanged a glance with her partner. "Do you feel dizzy? Any nausea?"

Becky swallowed hard. "A little."

"That's normal after a shock like this," Susan reassured her. "You might have a mild concussion. We can take you to the hospital to get checked out."

Becky shook her head quickly, the motion making her regret it immediately. "No. No hospital."

Susan hesitated. "Becky, you—"

"I'm fine," Becky cut in, her voice stronger this time. She didn't know what she was afraid of more—the sterile, fluorescent-lit halls of the ER or the idea of being alone with her thoughts. "Just... I need to know what happens next."

Susan didn't look convinced, but before she could argue, the crunch of tires against wet pavement signaled the arrival of another vehicle.

The police.

Arrival of Officers Delaney & Carter

The squad car rolled to a stop, its headlights cutting through the thick curtain of rain like twin beacons. The red and blue emergency lights pulsed against the slick pavement, painting the drenched road in shifting hues of crimson and sapphire. As the vehicle idled, its windshield wipers swiped back and forth with slow, mechanical precision, battling the endless drizzle.

Then, the front doors swung open, and two officers stepped out.

The first was Officer Delaney. He was a man who carried himself with the weight of experience, his broad-shouldered frame wrapped in a dark rain-slicked uniform that clung to him in the misty air. He was in his early forties, maybe late thirties, but the lines around his eyes made him look older—deep creases carved by long nights and years of witnessing the worst humanity had to offer. His features were strong and weathered, a square jaw covered in a faint layer of stubble. His dark brown hair was cropped close to his scalp, just beginning to pepper with gray at the temples. Even in the dim light, there was a sharpness in his gaze, his deep-set eyes a piercing shade of steely gray, scanning the scene with quiet calculation. He radiated the kind of authority that didn't need to be forced—he simply existed with the unshakable presence of a man who had seen everything and no longer had the luxury of being surprised.

Then there was Officer Carter.

He was younger—mid-to-late twenties at most—tall and lean but not scrawny, the kind of build that suggested he had once been an athlete but had let the discipline of training slip away over the years. His uniform fit a little too perfectly, his badge gleaming a little too brightly, marking him as someone who still carried the naivety of new blood. His face was all sharp angles—a defined jawline, high cheekbones, and eyes that might have been blue or green, though in the flickering lights they seemed colorless. His short, sandy-blond hair was neatly styled, though the rain had already begun to plaster it to his forehead. There was an unmistakable impatience in his movements, the way he adjusted his belt as if eager to prove himself, to do something—anything that was not just another routine accident report.

Carter let out a low whistle as he took in the wreckage. "Jesus. Another one?" His tone carried a thin layer of disbelief, but also something else—exasperation.

Delaney exhaled through his nose, rubbing a hand over his stubbled jaw. He was used to late-night calls, used to tragic accidents, but something about this one unsettled him. He was not sure if it was the way Becky stood at the edge of the scene, eyes wide and haunted, or if it was the way the rain made the blood on the pavement swirl into something almost surreal.

"You act like it's your first one," Delaney muttered.

Carter shrugged, stuffing his hands into his belt. "Yeah, well, most do not involve people *losing their heads*." His eyes flicked toward the sprawled body in the road, his lip curling slightly. "Literally."

Delaney shot him a look. "Show some respect."

Carter huffed but didn't argue. Instead, he flipped open his notepad, already scribbling. "Alright, let's see what the driver has to say."

Delaney nodded and turned toward Becky.

As he approached, his boots splashed through shallow puddles, the heavy thump-thump of his steps measured, deliberate. His expression remained unreadable, but there was something in the way his eyes lingered on her face—on the way her hands trembled against the thin blanket wrapped around her shoulders.

He had seen that kind of look before.

It was not just *shock*.

It was something else.

Something deeper.

Something wrong.

He crouched slightly to meet her gaze, his voice calm but firm.

"Ma'am," he said. "I'm Officer Delaney. Can you tell me what happened here?"

Becky swallowed, her throat raw. "I was driving home. It was raining—hard. A dog ran out into the road, and I swerved..." She sucked in a shaky breath. "And then he was just there. I didn't see him until it was too late."

Delaney nodded, his eyes steady on hers. "You hit the brakes?"

"Immediately," she whispered. "But it was too late."

He glanced at the wrecked front of her car, then back at her. "Were you alone in the vehicle?"

"Yes."

"No alcohol or drugs tonight?"

Becky shook her head. "I was not drinking. I was not distracted. I—" Her voice caught. "I just didn't see him."

Delaney studied her, then exchanged a brief glance with Carter, who stood a few feet away, scribbling notes on his notepad. The younger officer shot him a look that said, *This does not add up.*

Becky picked up on it. Her pulse quickened. "You do not believe me."

Delaney exhaled, his expression unreadable. "Ma'am, I believe you are telling me what you remember."

Becky frowned. "What's that supposed to mean?"

Delaney hesitated, then motioned toward the body. "The way he landed... it does not make sense."

Becky followed his gaze despite herself—and immediately regretted it.

His body. His head. Still there, still wrong.

She clenched her jaw, tearing her gaze away. "It does not make sense to me either."

Delaney watched her for a moment longer before nodding. "Alright, Becky. we are going to need a full statement. I need you to walk me through exactly what happened, step by step."

Becky exhaled shakily, rubbing her arms against the cold. "I already told you everything."

Delaney's tone softened, but he didn't relent. "Then tell me again."

Becky closed her eyes for a moment, summoning the strength to relive it.

The rain. The dog. The impossible way he appeared. The way he had looked at her.

She opened her eyes, locking onto Delaney's steady gaze.

"I think he was already dead before I hit him."

Silence.

Delaney's jaw tightened. Carter stopped scribbling.

And in the distance, the rain kept falling.

The Dashcam Footage & Investigation

A heavy silence stretched between them, broken only by the rain drumming against the asphalt. Becky's words hung in the air like an unspoken curse.

"I think he was already dead before I hit him."

Officer Delaney's jaw tightened. Carter had stopped writing, his notepad hanging limply in his hands.

Carter was the first to speak, his voice laced with disbelief. "you are saying you hit a dead man?" He let out a short, humorless laugh, shaking his head. "Jesus Christ."

Becky swallowed against the lump in her throat. "I—I do not know how else to explain it," she whispered.

Delaney studied her for a long moment, his expression unreadable. Then, without a word, he turned to Carter. "Check the dashcam."

Carter blinked. "What?"

"The dashcam," Delaney repeated, his voice firm. "Newer models have them built in. If she has one, it might've caught the whole thing."

Becky's breath hitched. She hadn't even thought about that.

Carter muttered something under his breath and stomped toward the wrecked vehicle, yanking open the driver's side door. He leaned in, shifting through the console. His fingers brushed against something small and rectangular, barely visible beneath the shattered remains of the windshield.

"Bingo," he muttered.

He pulled out the SD card and slipped it into a small tablet. The screen flickered to life.

Delaney and Becky crowded around him, the rain blurring the edges of their breath as Carter rewound the footage. The screen displayed nothing but the rain-slick road, the wipers moving frantically, the occasional flicker of lightning illuminating the dense trees lining the road.

"Alright," Carter muttered. "Let's see what the hell happened."

He fast-forwarded slightly—then suddenly, a blur darted into the road. Becky's recorded voice crackled through the tiny speakers:

"Shit—oh fuck—no, no, no—!"

The footage showed her hands wrenching the wheel to the left. The car skidded violently, the tires struggling against the wet pavement. The dashcam jolted as the car spun, headlights flickering over the rain-drenched road.

And then—

He appeared.

In one frame, there was nothing but rain.

In the next, he was *there*.

Standing perfectly still in the exact center of the road, his hands buried in the pockets of his hoodie.

His hood was up, casting a shadow over his face—but it did nothing to hide his piercing green eyes.

Eyes that stared directly into the camera.

Becky let out a shaky breath. Her entire body was trembling.

Carter muttered, "Holy shit."

The dashcam caught everything—the way Becky's car swerved, the moment of impact, the sheer force launching the man into the air. His body hit the hood hard, rolling up and across the windshield in a split second—

And just before he was flung out of frame—

The screen froze.

His face.

His smile.

Delaney's hand hovered over the tablet, his thumb hesitating over the playback button.

"...Zoom in," he murmured.

Carter did as he was told.

The grainy image sharpened slightly, and there it was—undeniable.

The man's lips were curved upward in a faint, knowing smile.

His green eyes—vivid, almost glowing in the headlights—locked onto the lens.

Even as his body crumpled.

Even as he was hit with lethal force.

He had been smiling.

Becky clutched the edges of the thin blanket wrapped around her shoulders, her breath shallow. "No. No, no, no. That's not possible."

Carter looked pale, his bravado from earlier evaporated. "That's not—" He shook his head. "How the hell—?"

Delaney finally pressed play again.

The man's body continued its arc, flung out of the frame.

Silence stretched between them.

Carter rubbed his temple. "Alright," he said hoarsely. "Let's check where the body landed."

The Perimeter Search

The rain had lightened to a mist as Delaney and Carter approached the site where the body had landed. His form was still, limbs bent at impossible angles against the wet pavement.

But what lay a few feet away kept Becky's eyes fixed on the road.

His head.

Becky turned away, bile rising in her throat.

"We need to check the perimeter," Delaney said, his voice unnaturally calm. "If he was not dead before the impact, something else did the job."

Carter, still rattled from the dashcam footage, let out a slow exhale and nodded.

The two officers swept their flashlights across the slick ground, their beams cutting through the thick fog rolling in from the woods.

Then, Carter's flashlight caught something in the tall grass just off the road—a thin, nearly invisible metal wire, strung taut between two wooden fence posts.

"Delaney," he called.

Delaney approached, crouching near the fence line. His gloved fingers brushed against the wire, and even in the dim light, he could see the faint sheen of blood glistening along its length.

"This is it," Delaney muttered.

Carter let out a low whistle. "Jesus. He must've landed neck-first. That's why the head..." He swallowed thickly. "Why it came off clean."

Becky, standing a few feet away, barely registered their words.

Her mind was still replaying the impossible.

The green eyes.

The smile.

The way he had been waiting.

Becky is Cleared

Delaney straightened, turning to Becky.

"Becky," he started carefully, "this was a freak accident."

She didn't move.

"You hit him, yes," Delaney continued, his voice steady but firm. "But he was alive when it happened. He was not dead before impact." He gestured toward the wire fence. "That's what severed his head."

Becky's lips parted, but no words came.

"It was not your fault," Delaney said, softer now. "I know how bad this looks, how it must feel, but there are no criminal wrongdoings here."

Becky's throat tightened. She wanted to believe him.

Wanted to take his words and let them wash away the crushing weight pressing against her ribs.

But she couldn't forget those eyes.

That smile.

And most of all—

The way he had been waiting.

Delaney must have sensed her hesitation because he sighed and reached into his pocket, pulling out a small white card. He held it out to her.

"My contact information," he said. "If you remember anything else, or if you just need to talk, call me."

Becky took it with numb fingers. "Thanks."

Becky Leaves the Scene

The flashing lights of the patrol cars and ambulance cast eerie reflections on the wet pavement, dancing in red and blue streaks across the puddles. The rain had slowed to a whisper, a mere echo of the storm's earlier fury. The air smelled of damp asphalt, metal, and something else—something she couldn't name.

Becky stood at the edge of the scene, arms wrapped tightly around herself, as if holding herself together. Her mind was a cacophony of noise and silence all at once, the remnants of adrenaline still pulsing beneath her skin. She was here, standing, breathing—but part of her still felt caught in the moment of impact, the shuddering crash looping behind her eyes.

Officer Delaney turned to her with a firm yet understanding expression. "A tow truck will be here soon to take your car to the station until the investigation is officially completed. If there's anything you need to grab from it, now's the time."

Becky hesitated, her gaze drifting toward the wreckage. Her car looked eerily lifeless under the flickering streetlights, as if the accident had drained it of any purpose beyond the crumpled shape it had become.

She swallowed, forcing her legs to move. Each step toward the car felt heavier than the last, like wading through water. Leaning inside, she let her fingers brush against the interior—cold, damp, unfamiliar.

Her hand found the strap of her purse, and she pulled it toward her, hesitating for just a moment before slinging it over her shoulder. The scent of gasoline and rain filled her nose, stirring a fresh wave of unease.

She stepped back.

"That's all I need," she murmured, not sparing the car another glance.

"You sure you do not need a ride home?" Delaney asked.

Becky shook her head, rubbing her hands together for warmth. "I'll call a cab."

He studied her for a moment, then nodded. He would not push. "Take care of yourself, Becky."

She didn't answer.

Instead, she pulled her phone from her damp pocket, fingers stiff from the cold, and called for a cab. Her voice sounded distant, hollow. As she ended the call, she exhaled a slow, shaky breath, watching it curl into the night air.

She didn't know if she was cold from the weather—

Or from something else entirely.

Ten minutes later, a dull yellow sedan pulled up to the edge of the scene. Its headlights flickered slightly as it idled, waiting.

Becky took a deep breath, exhaling slowly, and walked toward it.

The cab was old—the kind that had seen too many miles and too few repairs. As Becky pulled the heavy door open, the hinges groaned in protest, a sound swallowed by the steady patter of rain. The faded yellow exterior was speckled with droplets, the paint dull beneath the hazy glow of the streetlights. The windshield wipers moved sluggishly, leaving faint streaks across the glass, as though the machine itself was as tired as its driver.

She slid into the backseat, and the door shut with a dull thud—a sound that seemed far too final. The interior smelled of stale cigarettes, old vinyl, and the faintest trace of cheap pine air freshener. A single black tree-shaped freshener dangled limply from the rearview mirror, barely clinging to its last vestiges of scent. The seats were cracked leather, the kind that stuck to the skin if one sat there long enough. The faint scent of sweat and something vaguely greasy lingered in the air, mixing with the dampness that clung to Becky's clothes.

The cab was dimly lit, the only real glow coming from the dashboard—a flickering green light from the meter, which ticked up in slow increments. The driver's radio was on, but the volume was barely audible, playing some kind of soft, crackling talk radio station that cut in and out with static, as if the storm had disrupted the signal. She could make out a voice, low and monotonous, speaking about the stock market, the rising cost of gas, and a recent UFO sighting—a mix of dull and bizarre that barely registered in her exhausted mind.

The driver, a middle-aged man with deep lines carved into his face, barely spared her a glance in the rearview mirror as he reached for the gearshift. His tired eyes, dark and sunken, flickered over her reflection before settling back on the road. He had graying stubble along his jaw and deep bags beneath his eyes, the kind of weary expression that suggested he had been driving this cab for far too many years and had long since stopped caring about conversation. His uniform—a plain, faded blue button-up—was slightly wrinkled, and a half-finished Styrofoam cup of coffee sat precariously in the cup holder.

"Rough night?" he asked, his voice gravelly and worn. Not exactly concerned, just... making conversation out of obligation.

Becky didn't answer.

She buckled herself in and stared out the rain-streaked window.

"Where to?" the driver prompted.

Becky gave him her address, her voice barely above a whisper.

The cab pulled away, the flashing lights of the accident scene fading into the distance.

The driver made a few attempts at small talk, but Becky ignored him.

Instead, she kept her eyes fixed on the darkened streets, the rain-soaked roads stretching ahead like an endless void.

She wanted to believe it was over.

That it really had just been a freak accident.

But as the cab rolled past the empty sidewalks and darkened store-fronts, she couldn't shake the feeling that somewhere out there...

Those green eyes were still watching.

CHAPTER FIVE

A Ride Home in Silence

Neighborhood in the Rain

The rain had softened into a whisper by the time Becky's cab pulled into the outskirts of her neighborhood. Even through her haze of exhaustion, she recognized the dimly lit streets, the familiar silhouettes of houses lined in uneven rows, their windows dark and lifeless. The world here was asleep, untouched by the horrors she carried with her.

Each house sat nestled within the skeletal grip of towering oak and maple trees, their branches still dripping from the storm. Some homes had small porches with sagging steps; others bore the remnants of peeling white picket fences. The cracked sidewalks and occasional flickering streetlights only added to the eerie quiet that had settled over the area.

It was the kind of neighborhood that always looked damp, even on dry days. Time had pressed its weight into the streets, leaving behind cracked pavement and rusted mailboxes leaning at odd angles. Some yards had toys left forgotten in the grass, water pooling around them, their owners long since tucked into warm beds.

It was deceptively normal.

Safe.

But tonight, it felt like a place frozen in time—a world separate from the one Becky had just left.

She watched the houses pass by in a blur, her stomach twisting. She wondered if any of the sleeping souls inside would wake up in the morning and feel what she felt now. Would they step outside and sense that something in the air had changed? Would they notice the way the world had tilted, just slightly, out of its natural rhythm?

Or was she the only one?

A Moving Coffin

Inside the cab, the air was thick with the stale remnants of old cigarettes and artificial pine-scented air freshener. The scent clung to the cracked leather seats, settled deep into the worn fabric, mixing with something else—something damp, like rain-soaked upholstery that had never fully dried. It made Becky's stomach twist, nausea curling deep within her gut.

The ceiling was lined with a thin layer of dust, barely visible in the dim interior light. A frayed tassel from a past air freshener dangled from the rearview mirror, swaying slightly with each turn the car made.

The driver's seat was pushed forward just enough that she could see the back of the man's head—short-cropped hair, thinning near the temples, speckled with gray. His shoulders were broad, his thick hands gripping the wheel with the kind of ease that came from decades of late-night shifts.

The radio was on but faint, almost ghostlike, playing an old rock ballad that crackled with static, its melody barely discernible beneath the rhythmic sweep of the windshield wipers. The sound blended into the low hum of the engine, turning the atmosphere inside the cab into something unsettlingly detached.

Becky pressed herself into the cold leather seat, her head resting against the damp window. Rain still trickled down the glass in slow, lazy trails, catching the streetlights in fractured veins of gold. The effect was almost hypnotic, a quiet illusion that made the world outside feel far away—like she was not really here, like none of this was real.

Maybe it was not.

Maybe she was still standing on that road, staring at his body.

Maybe she never left.

The thought sent a fresh jolt of nausea through her.

Unspoken Questions

The driver, for the most part, remained silent. His focus was fixed on the road, but Becky could feel his occasional glances through the rearview mirror—small, fleeting moments of curiosity, of unspoken questions.

Where had she been?

Why did she look like that?

What the hell had happened to her?

She didn't care.

She was not sure she could speak even if she wanted to.

A sudden pothole jolted her, pulling her from the edge of thought. The driver muttered something under his breath, adjusting his grip on the wheel.

Then, without looking at her, he spoke.

"Long night, huh?"

His voice was gruff but not unkind. A question wrapped in casual indifference, the way someone might comment on the weather. But underneath it, there was something else—a curiosity laced with caution, with concern.

Becky's throat tightened. She couldn't answer. The words felt trapped inside her, buried beneath the weight of everything she had seen.

The driver glanced at her again in the mirror, his thick brows furrowing slightly. "Alright then. One of those nights."

His fingers tapped against the steering wheel, keeping time with the radio's faint melody. The wipers swished, swished, and swished, a rhythmic metronome against the glass.

Becky barely heard it.

All she could hear was the wet thud of impact.

The crunch of bone.

The way his body had twisted, unnatural, broken.

And the worst part—the part that made her stomach lurch every time she thought of it—

He had been smiling.

CHAPTER SIX

Home, but Not Safe

A House that Waited

When the cab finally slowed to a stop, Becky felt the weight of her own house looming before her.

It stood just as she had left it—small, unassuming, deceptively normal. The kind of house that didn't belong to someone with secrets. A modest, single-story home with faded blue siding and a porch light that flickered slightly, the bulb on the verge of dying. The paint along the edges of the front door had begun to peel, and the wooden steps creaked under even the slightest pressure.

It was a house that belonged to someone ordinary.

Not to someone who had left behind a body in the rain.

Not to someone who couldn't shake the feeling that something had followed her home.

Becky fumbled in her pocket, fingers brushing against damp fabric, pulling out a crumpled twenty. She shoved it toward the driver, her voice barely above a whisper.

"Keep it."

The man hesitated, his gaze lingering on her longer than necessary. She could feel him studying her, assessing her. Maybe he thought she had just come from a bad date. Maybe he thought she had been drinking, stumbling home after one too many.

But she could tell—he knew it was something else.

He didn't press.

He took the bill and stuffed it into the cup holder. "Alright. Have a good night."

She didn't respond.

She shoved the door open and stepped out into the drizzle.

The cab's headlights flickered as the driver reversed out of the drive-

way. His taillights glowed red, a fleeting pulse of life before disappearing into the mist.

And then she was alone.

The world was quiet now.

The silence pressed against her ears, heavy and unnatural.

She stood there for a long moment, staring at the front door, her hand
gripping the keys so tightly the ridges bit into her palm.

Something felt wrong.

She was not supposed to be here.

She was not supposed to have made it home.

Her breath hitched, the thought slamming into her with the force
of a cold hand around her throat. The night air was damp, but it was
not what made her shiver. Hadn't she felt it, even before she reached
the house? That prickling sensation at the base of her neck, the weight
of unseen eyes?

Her fingers fumbled at the lock. The key slipped once, twice.

This was not relief. This was not safety.

She had made it home.

But something—someone—had expected her not to.

Inside, but Not Alone

The moment she stepped inside, she knew.

Nothing obvious—no shattered windows, no gaping doors swinging open. But something was off. The air felt thick, almost stagnant, as if the house itself had been holding its breath.

The faint scent of lavender still clung to the space, just as she had left it. But underneath it, something else. Something metallic. Something stale.

Her gaze swept over the living room. Everything looked the same. The blanket draped over the couch, unmoved. Her half-empty coffee mug sat on the table, untouched.

But the door to her bedroom—

It was open. Just an inch.

Becky always closed it before leaving.

A slow prickle crawled up her spine. Did she forget? No. She was sure she hadn't.

She swallowed hard, forcing herself to move. The floorboards groaned beneath her weight, the sound splintering through the silence.

Her hand hovered over the door handle. Her breath hitched.

One sharp exhale. Then she pushed.

Darkness.

The glow of the streetlights barely bled through the curtains, casting faint, jagged shadows across the floor.

Nothing looked disturbed.

But she felt it.

Something had been there.

Or worse—

Something still was.

The Weight of Exhaustion

Becky peeled off her damp hoodie, the fabric clinging to her skin as if resisting her touch. It fell to the floor in a limp heap. She rubbed her arms, trying to chase away the chill that had settled deep into her bones.

Her body felt heavy, sluggish. Like she was carrying something unseen.

Her fingers twitched as she reached for the light switch in the bathroom. The bulb flickered once before steadying, casting an unforgiving glare across the mirror.

She barely recognized herself.

Her skin was pale, her eyes hollow. Shadows pooled beneath them, deep and unyielding. The remnants of dried rain clung to her hair, dark strands curling against her temples. She reached up, hesitating before touching her own reflection.

Becky looked away first.

The shower should have been comforting, washing away the night's horrors. But as the hot water cascaded over her skin, she couldn't shake the feeling that she shouldn't be doing this—that something about this routine felt wrong.

She had stood over a dead man's body tonight.

She had seen his head, separate from his body.

She had seen him smile.

And now she was just... standing in her shower?

The thought turned her stomach. She shut the water off abruptly, her breath coming in shallow, uneven gasps.

Sleep, or Something Like It

The bedroom still felt off, but exhaustion outweighed fear.

   She climbed into bed, the sheets cool against her damp skin. The weight of the blanket should have been comforting, grounding. Instead, it felt suffocating, like being buried beneath something heavy and unseen.

   She curled in on herself, tucking her knees to her chest. She told herself she would stay awake. Just for a little while. Just to make sure she was alone.

   But her body betrayed her.

   Sleep took hold before she could fight it.

   And just before the darkness claimed her, Becky swore she heard it.

   A whisper of movement.

   A presence.

   Watching.

   Waiting.

   She didn't wake up.

   She couldn't.

   The house made sure of that.

CHAPTER SEVEN

The Night That Changed Everything

.

A Knock in the Dark

The rain had slowed to a whisper against the roof, but the silence inside Becky's house felt suffocating. The dim glow of her bedside clock read 2:47 AM, casting faint blue light across the room. Clothes lay crumpled on the chair, her blanket twisted in a heap, and her laptop sat on the desk, screen dark. Everything was exactly as she had left it.

But she had no memory of the past few days.

Becky's fingers tightened around the sheets. Her head ached—not a sharp pain, but a deep, dull throbbing like she had been holding her breath for too long. Her mouth was dry, her limbs heavy, and the sensation of being somewhere she didn't belong wrapped around her like a vice. She swallowed, trying to remember what she had done yesterday.

Nothing came.

I should call Aaron, she thought, suddenly feeling the weight of silence. She didn't usually check in with him first thing in the morning, but after last night... she just wanted to hear a familiar voice.

He lost someone in a car accident Years ago, before they were friends. He never talked about it much, but Becky had caught glimpses of it—how his jaw would tighten when sirens blared in the distance, how he always insisted on driving whenever they went out at night.

And now, she had nearly hit someone too.

She rubbed her arms, suddenly chilled.

She had her phone in hand, ready to call Aaron, when she heard it.

A sharp knock at the door. The sudden sound sent a violent jolt through her body.

Becky sat up, heart hammering. She strained to listen, her breath shallow.

Another knock. Louder. More insistent.

She lurched out of bed, her bare feet hitting the cold floor, but she hesitated before reaching for the doorknob.

Then—

"Becky? You in there?"

Her stomach unclenched at the familiar voice. Aaron.

Relief mixed with lingering unease as she unlocked the door and pulled it open. Aaron stood outside, rain-drenched and breathless, his dark hoodie clinging to his frame. He looked her over with a deep crease between his brows. "Jesus, Beck. I've been calling you for two days."

Two days?

Becky blinked. Her grip on the doorknob tightened. "What...?"

Aaron stepped inside, shaking out his damp sleeves. "I thought something happened to you. You weren't answering your phone." He ran a hand through his rain-soaked hair. "Where the hell have you been?"

Becky didn't know how to answer. The words formed but refused to leave her mouth. What had she been doing?

She turned, scanning the living room. Everything was in place. The empty coffee mug from—whenever she had last been awake—still sat on the counter. The blanket she usually left on the couch was folded neatly, which she never did. And her phone—

Her gaze darted to the coffee table. Her phone lay there, undisturbed.

Aaron followed her stare and exhaled. "Beck, what's going on?"

She swallowed hard. "I do not know."

Fragments of Time

Aaron sat on the couch, watching her closely. Becky stood frozen, trying to force her brain to rewind, to find anything solid to hold onto. But when she closed her eyes, she didn't get memories.

She got flashes.

She saw herself moving through the house, but everything was wrong—hazy, disjointed, like watching a film that kept skipping frames.

She was standing at the kitchen sink, but the faucet was running and overflowing, water spilling over her hands.

She was in bed, but something had woken her up, and she was staring at the ceiling, unblinking, unable to move.

She was at the front door—standing there for what felt like hours—listening.

A sharp shiver ran through her, and she wrapped her arms around herself. She knew this was not normal. She knew something had happened in the missing time.

But she didn't know what.

Aaron leaned forward, resting his elbows on his knees. "Did you go out? See anyone?"

"No."

"Did anyone come here?"

She hesitated. "...I do not think so."

Aaron's frown deepened. "Becky, this isn't like you."

She knew that.

But how did she explain something she didn't understand?

She sank onto the couch beside him, pressing the heels of her hands to her eyes. "I think I lost time."

Aaron stiffened. "Like... blackout?"

She exhaled shakily. "Like I was here, but I was not."

Aaron rubbed his jaw. "Jesus." He leaned back, staring at the ceiling. "Do you want to go to the hospital?"

"No." The answer came too fast, too forceful. Becky didn't trust hospitals. They would poke and prod, run tests, and send her home with no real answers. And worse—

She didn't want to hear what they might find.

Aaron sighed, but he didn't push. "Alright. But you are not staying here alone."

Becky didn't argue. She didn't want to be alone either.

The Unsettling Truth

Aaron made them tea. Becky sat curled up on the couch, hands wrapped around the warm mug, but the chill in her bones would not leave.

She thought about checking her phone, scrolling through texts or calls to see if there was anything she had missed. But the thought of seeing blank days in her log made her stomach turn. If there was nothing there—if there was no proof she had existed during those missing hours—it would be worse.

Then, a sinking realization hit her.

Her article.

Her deadline.

Becky bolted upright, her mug nearly slipping from her grasp. "No. No, no, no."

Aaron frowned. "What?"

"My article," she whispered. "I had a deadline. Monday." She scrambled to her laptop, fingers shaking as she pulled up her inbox.

Her heart sank. The email reminder was there, bold and mocking.

Due: Monday.

It was now Thursday.

"Shit," she breathed, running a hand through her hair. "They're going to kill me."

Aaron didn't hesitate. He grabbed her phone. "Who's your contact?"

Becky hesitated. "Jules Merritt."

He scrolled through the contacts until he found J.M. and hit call.

Becky stared at him, wide-eyed, as he pressed the phone to his ear.

After a moment, someone picked up.

"Hey, Jules? This is Aaron, Becky's friend." His tone was smooth, professional—almost too good. "Listen, Becky was in an accident, and she's just now realizing she missed her deadline. She's a wreck about it."

Becky bit her lip, watching him with a mix of awe and dread.

There was a pause, then a sharp reply from the other end.

Aaron's expression remained neutral, though his jaw tightened. "Yeah, I get it. But look, you know how reliable she is. This was out of her hands. She just needs a little time to get back on track. Can you give her an extension?"

Another pause.

Aaron nodded. "Understood. She'll have it to you by the weekend. Thanks, Jules. Really."

He hung up and turned to Becky. "You've got until Saturday. Jules isn't happy, but they'll live."

Becky exhaled in relief, dropping her head into her hands. "you are a lifesaver."

Aaron smirked. "Yeah, yeah. Just do not make a habit of it."

Then, he leaned back against the couch. "I'm staying here tonight."

Becky looked at him, about to argue, but the exhaustion in her body said otherwise.

"Okay."

Outside, the storm raged on, but inside, for the first time in days, Becky felt grounded.

The Weight of the Truth

The living room was dimly lit, the single floor lamp casting a golden haze over the space, stretching its shadows long against the walls. The air inside was stale, unmoving—like the house itself had been frozen in time since the accident.

Aaron's presence felt too big in the quiet, his movements careful as he set a takeout bag on the coffee table, his fingers still curled around the handle like he didn't quite trust the room to be real.

He turned to her, his posture rigid, the silence between them stretching impossibly thin. "You didn't answer your phone."

She flinched.

The guilt settled deep in her chest. She could feel his gaze on her—sharp, assessing.

"I..." She swallowed, her voice dry, barely audible. "I didn't know what to say."

Aaron's brows furrowed. His hands flexed at his sides, fingers twitching as if he wanted to reach for her but was not sure if he should. "Tell me now."

Becky exhaled shakily, sinking onto the couch, her legs pulling up against her chest as if she could fold in on herself.

Then, she told him.

She told him everything.

At first, the words came in broken fragments—halting, unsure, her voice trembling under the weight of the memory. The rain. The dark road. The dog. And then... him.

Her voice shook as she spoke, every word pulling her back to that night.

The storm. The wet pavement. The way the headlights had sliced through the darkness just long enough to illuminate him.

Aaron sat beside her on the couch, silent, unmoving. His jaw tightened when she described the impact—the way the man's body had flown like a discarded puppet. But when she told him about his head... about the way it had landed, separate from his body, and staring back at her... smiling—

Aaron inhaled sharply. His hands curled into fists on his knees, but he didn't interrupt.

But he never interrupted.

When she finally whispered, "I still see him."

Aaron tensed.

"...In reflections. In my window. He's still there, Aaron."

Silence.

Aaron sat in stunned silence, his face pale. He wanted to be skeptical. She could see it in the way his jaw tightened, the way his fingers laced together as if grounding himself.

But he believed her.

Not because the story made sense, but because she was Becky.

And Becky didn't lie.

When she finished, she was shaking, her breath unsteady, and Aaron didn't hesitate. He reached for her, pulling her against him, his arms wrapping around her shoulders.

She sank into him, clutching at his sweater as if he were the only thing keeping her from shattering.

"I've got you," he murmured against her hair.

And for the first time since that night, Becky felt safe.

A Moment of Vulnerability

Becky exhaled shakily, wiping at her damp face with the heel of her palm. The weight of exhaustion clung to her limbs, sinking into her bones like an anchor. "I... I think I need a shower," she murmured, her voice barely more than a breath. "I just— I feel gross. I haven't..." Her words trailed off, swallowed by the lump forming in her throat. Embarrassment prickled at the edges of her vulnerability.

Aaron nodded, his gaze steady as he stood. "Go ahead. I'll be here when you get out."

She turned toward the hallway, pausing at the threshold as something cold and uncertain coiled inside her chest. The silence felt too vast, too empty, stretching between them like a yawning chasm.

"Aaron?" The whisper barely made it past her lips.

He looked up immediately, concern flickering in his expression. "Yeah?"

She hesitated, pressing her nails into her palm. "...Can you stay close?"

Surprise flitted across his face, quickly chased by understanding. His features softened, and he gave her a small, reassuring nod. "Of course."

Becky swallowed against the tightness in her throat, shifting her weight. Then, more hesitantly, she added, "Can you... come in?"

Aaron stilled, the muscles in his jaw tightening almost imperceptibly. "Inside?"

She nodded, her cheeks heating. The idea felt ridiculous when spoken aloud, but the thought of being alone right now—of standing under the spray with nothing but her own thoughts—sent an uneasy shiver up her spine.

"I do not want to feel alone," she admitted. "You do not have to look or anything, just... be there."

His throat bobbed as he swallowed hard, his knuckles briefly flexing at his sides. There was a hesitation—a flicker of something unreadable in his eyes—but then he gave a sharp nod.

"Okay."

The Shower

The bathroom filled with the hiss of steaming water, the air turning thick with the scent of lavender body wash and something faintly metallic from the old pipes. Condensation clung to the mirror, distorting their reflections in rippling streaks.

Aaron sat stiffly on the closed toilet lid, hands clasped between his knees, staring resolutely at the tile floor as if it held the secrets of the universe. The hum of the water and the occasional splash echoed in the small space, a barrier between them, yet his awareness of Becky's presence just beyond the thin shower curtain was suffocatingly acute.

She moved, and the water changed cadence, cascading against her skin in rhythmic sheets. He squeezed his eyes shut, exhaling slowly through his nose. This was fine. He was fine.

Then—"Aaron?"

His head snapped up instinctively. "Yeah?"

The curtain pulled back slightly, revealing a sliver of damp, glistening skin and a delicate, outstretched hand. "Towel?"

His breath hitched as he grabbed the fluffy white towel from the rack beside him, but in the briefest of moments—before he could stop himself—his gaze flicked downward. Just for a second. A single, fleeting second.

Then realization struck like a lightning bolt.

Heat exploded across his face as his head jerked back up, fingers tightening around the towel like it was a lifeline. Shit.

Becky caught the movement. She caught the hesitation. And then, much to his horror, she smirked.

"Aaron..."

His throat worked, his voice hoarse. "Yeah?"

Her gaze flicked downward, then back up, arching a perfectly knowing brow. "Is that a...?"

Aaron froze, following her gaze in delayed horror. The unmistakable tension in his jeans was suddenly impossible to ignore. His entire body locked up as if he'd been caught in a spotlight.

"Fuck." He thought to himself.

His face burned so hot he was certain he'd combust on the spot. "I—I'm gonna step out."

Becky's laughter echoed against the tiled walls, warm and unguarded. It was not mocking—just surprised, maybe a little amused—but the second Aaron all but tripped over himself in his haste to escape, her smile faltered.

"Aaron, wait." Becky called out.

He didn't. The door clicked shut behind him, and she heard his muffled groan from the other side. Becky sighed, running a hand through her damp hair. She hadn't meant to laugh like that. It was not funny—not in the way that made someone feel small. It was natural.

Human.

She pressed her lips together, then, after a moment, stepped out of the shower, droplets of water trickling down her skin as she grabbed the towel and wrapped it snugly around herself. The thick fabric clung to her, still warm from the heated air.

Taking a breath, she opened the door.

Aaron stood just outside, his back against the wall, arms folded tightly over his chest as if he were trying to shrink into himself. He didn't look at her immediately, his jaw tight, eyes fixed somewhere off to the side.

"Aaron."

His fingers twitched. "...Yeah?"

Becky took a small step forward, the damp tile cooling her bare feet. "I didn't mean to laugh at you." Her voice was soft, patient. "You do not have to be embarrassed."

Aaron let out a short, self-conscious breath, shaking his head. "I—I know, I just—" He dragged a hand through his hair, exhaling hard. "I was not expecting that to happen. And you... I mean, you noticed. Obviously."

She smiled gently. "It's normal, Aaron."

His eyes flicked to her, cautious, still a little unsure.

"Really," she reassured him, stepping closer. "You stayed. You did what I asked, and I really appreciate that." Her fingers curled into the edge of the towel, holding it in place. "You do not have to feel weird about it."

Aaron swallowed, his gaze finally meeting hers fully. There was still the faintest hint of pink in his cheeks, but something in his posture eased.

Becky tilted her head toward the bedroom. "Come on?"

Aaron hesitated, but then, nodding slowly, he followed her down the hall. His steps were a little slower, his embarrassment still lingered in the way he carried himself. But Becky didn't push.

As they reached the room, she bumped her shoulder lightly against his, a small, wordless gesture of comfort.

Aaron huffed out a breath—half amusement, half something else.

He still felt awkward. But maybe, just maybe, not as much.

The Breaking Point

The tension had been building all night.

Not just tonight, though. Years.

Unspoken words, lingering glances, touches that lasted just a moment too long—every fleeting second between them had led to this. And now, as Becky sat beside Aaron on her bed, wrapped in a towel with damp hair clinging to her shoulders, she felt the weight of it pressing against her chest, making it harder to breathe.

Aaron had always been steady, unwavering, her anchor in every storm. But now, there was something different in the way he looked at her. A quiet intensity, as if he could feel it too—the invisible pull between them, the way the air seemed thicker, charged with something neither of them had dared acknowledge before.

She reached for his hand, fingers curling around his. It was a simple gesture, but it sent a shiver up her spine. His skin was warm, his thumb brushing instinctively over her knuckles, soothing yet electrifying all at once.

"Aaron..." Her voice was barely above a whisper, hesitant but certain.

His gaze lifted to hers, searching. "Yeah?"

She hesitated, her heart pounding. She didn't want to second-guess this—not tonight, not anymore. "Stay with me."

Aaron's brows furrowed slightly. "I told you, I'm not going anywhere."

"No, I mean..." She swallowed hard, shifting closer. Her fingers tightened around his. "Really stay with me."

Understanding flickered in his eyes, followed almost instantly by uncertainty. "Becky, are you sure?" His voice was hoarse now, careful, as if he was terrified of misinterpreting what she was asking.

She nodded, her breath unsteady. "I've always wanted this, Aaron." The words spilled out before she could stop them, but she didn't regret them. They were true. "Even if tonight never happened... Even if I wasn't a mess... I still would've wanted this."

Aaron let out a breath like he'd been holding it for years. His fingers slid into her hair, his touch gentle, reverent. "You mean that?"

Becky nodded, her chest rising and falling rapidly. "I do."

And then he kissed her.

Soft at first, hesitant—like he was afraid she'd change her mind. But the moment her fingers tangled in his hair, pulling him closer, that hesitation vanished. The kiss deepened, slow but desperate, his lips molding perfectly against hers. His hands found her waist, pulling her against him as if he'd been waiting his whole life to hold her like this.

Becky melted into him, the warmth of his body seeping into hers, grounding her in ways she hadn't thought possible. She had spent days drowning in fear and guilt, but now, in Aaron's arms, she felt alive.

His hands roamed up her back, slow and careful, as if memorizing every curve. When his fingers brushed the knot of her towel, a quiet gasp left her lips. She felt him tense beneath her, pulling back just slightly, his forehead pressing against hers.

"We do not have to rush," he murmured, breathless.

"I do not want to stop," she whispered back, her fingers trailing down the front of his shirt. "I need this. I need you."

Aaron exhaled shakily, his resolve breaking. His hands slid to the edge of her towel, pulling it away in one fluid motion. He paused when she was bare before him, his gaze flickering over her with something between awe and restraint.

"God, Becky…" His voice was thick with emotion, his fingertips tracing the smooth line of her collarbone before dipping lower.

She shivered under his touch, arching instinctively into him. His hands were warm, his palms rough but gentle as they cupped her breasts, his thumbs brushing over her sensitive peaks. A soft moan escaped her lips, and she felt Aaron shudder at the sound.

"you are beautiful," he murmured, almost like he couldn't believe she was real.

Becky smiled, a slow, knowing curve of her lips. "Then show me."

That was all it took.

Aaron's restraint snapped like a thread pulled too tight. His mouth was on hers again, hungry, desperate, and full of everything they had both been holding back for years. His kisses trailed from her lips down to her neck, then her breasts, then stomach, lower still, his mouth leaving a burning path against her skin.

Becky's body responded to every touch, every caress. She tugged at his shirt, impatient, needing to feel him against her. He obliged, pulling it over his head before pressing her back against the bed. His weight on top of her was perfect, solid, real.

Fingers explored, mouths collided, bodies tangled. Every touch, every sigh, every whispered name sent heat spiraling through her, coiling low in her stomach. Aaron's hands gripped her thighs, spreading them apart as he settled between them, his breath ragged against her ear.

"Tell me you want this," he rasped.

Becky met his gaze, her own dark with need. "I've never wanted anything more."

That was all he needed.

His lips crashed against hers as he pushed inside her, slow and deep, filling her completely. Becky gasped, her nails digging into his shoulders as pleasure bloomed through her, stealing her breath. Aaron groaned at the feeling of her wrapped around him, his head dropping against her shoulder as he fought for control.

They moved together, a rhythm that felt natural, inevitable—like they had always been meant to fit this way. His thrusts were slow at first, savoring the feeling, but as Becky's hands roamed down his back, pulling him closer, he lost himself in her.

Soft moans and whispered names filled the room, mingling with the sound of rain still pattering softly outside. Aaron's hands were everywhere—gripping her hips, sliding up her sides, threading through her hair. Every touch sent shivers through her, every movement pushing her closer to the edge.

Becky arched against him, meeting his thrusts, her breath coming in short, desperate gasps. "Aaron—" Her voice broke as pleasure built inside her, tight and overwhelming.

"I've got you," he whispered against her lips, his rhythm never faltering. "Let go."

And she did.

Slow, deep thrusts. Fingers tracing every inch of her. Lips claiming her as if she was the only thing that had ever mattered. Her body tensed before shattering completely, waves of bliss crashing through her.

And Becky let go, surrendering herself to Aaron completely—body, heart, soul.

When she cried out his name, trembling in pleasure, Aaron followed, burying himself in her as he whispered hers back like a prayer.

For a long time, they lay tangled together, their breathing the only sound in the quiet room. Becky traced slow, lazy circles along Aaron's spine, her heart still pounding, but this time not from fear.

Aaron pressed a soft kiss to her shoulder, his arms tightening around her as if he never wanted to let go. "You okay?" he murmured.

Becky smiled, warm and content, for the first time in what felt like forever. She tilted her head to look at him, brushing a strand of hair from his forehead.

"More than okay," she whispered.

Aaron exhaled, relief washing over his features. "Good."

He pulled her closer, tucking her against him, their bodies fitting together perfectly. The warmth of him, the steady sound of his breathing, the way his fingers lazily traced along her skin—it felt like home.

And as sleep finally began to pull her under, Becky realized that no matter what haunted her—no matter what waited for her in the dark—she was not alone anymore.

She had him.

CHAPTER EIGHT

Breakfast of Sufferers

Aaron sat on the couch, watching her closely. Becky stood frozen, trying to force her brain to rewind, to find anything solid to hold onto. But when she closed her eyes, she didn't get memories.

She got flashes.

She saw herself moving through the house, but everything was wrong—hazy, disjointed, like watching a film that kept skipping frames.

She was standing at the kitchen sink, but the faucet was running and overflowing, water spilling over her hands.

She was in bed, but something had woken her up, and she was staring at the ceiling, unblinking, unable to move.

She was at the front door—standing there for what felt like hours—listening.

A sharp shiver ran through her, and she wrapped her arms around herself. She knew this was not normal. She knew something had happened in the missing time.

But she didn't know what.

Aaron leaned forward, resting his elbows on his knees. "Did you go out? See anyone?"

"No."

"Did anyone come here?"

She hesitated. "...I do not think so."

Aaron's frown deepened. "Becky, this isn't like you."

She knew that.

But how did she explain something she didn't understand?

She sank onto the couch beside him, pressing the heels of her hands to her eyes. "I think I lost time."

Aaron stiffened. "Like... blackout?"

She exhaled shakily. "Like I was here, but I was not."

Aaron rubbed his jaw. "Jesus." He leaned back, staring at the ceiling. "Do you want to go to the hospital?"

"No." The answer came too fast, too forceful. Becky didn't trust hospitals. They would poke and prod, run tests, and send her home with no real answers. And worse—

She didn't want to hear what they might find.

Aaron sighed, but he didn't push. "Alright. But you are not staying here alone."

Becky didn't argue. She didn't want to be alone either.

A House Too Quiet

Becky's feet barely made a sound as she moved through the house, her mind spiraling further with each empty room.

The living room. The couch was still messy, the blankets crumpled where they had sat last night, but no sign of him.

The coffee table. Two forgotten water glasses. His sweatshirt, discarded.

But the room felt like a ghost of the night before, a hollow echo of what had been.

The walls seemed to breathe around her, expanding, shrinking.

Aaron was gone.

Her pulse thundered in her ears.

Had she only imagined it? Had her mind fabricated the warmth, the comfort, the way he held her as if nothing else mattered?

A horrifying thought struck her.

What if last night never happened?

Her breath hitched.

What if she had been alone this whole time? What if she had just convinced herself he was there because the alternative—being alone with her fear, her guilt, her ghosts—was too much to bear?

The weight in her chest pressed harder, threatening to crush her.

Then—

A sound.

Soft. Distant.

Movement.

A shift of weight. The faint clink of something settling on a hard surface.

Becky whirled toward the noise, her breath catching, her heart stumbling over itself in its frantic pace.

The panic was still lodged deep in her throat as she moved blindly, following the sound with single-minded desperation.

She reached the threshold, stepping into the kitchen—

And stopped.

Proof of Morning

Aaron stood in the soft light of morning, the golden glow spilling through the window, brushing against his features.

He was there.

Real. Solid. Whole.

A plate was balanced in one hand, a steaming mug in the other. He looked normal, calm—completely unaware of the storm that had nearly drowned her moments ago.

But what hit her the hardest—what made her breath shudder past her lips—was the way his eyes locked onto hers.

Dark. Concerned.

They took her in, absorbing the tension still clinging to her frame, the rapid rise and fall of her chest.

"Beck?"

His voice was soft, cautious.

Like he knew.

Like he could see the fear still wrapped around her like a vice, suffocating, crushing.

"What's wrong?"

Her hands trembled at her sides. She tried to answer, but the words caught in her throat, stuck somewhere between relief and residual panic.

"I..."

Her voice was barely there.

She had been so sure he was gone.

So sure she had woken up to a nightmare.

Aaron's brow furrowed deeper, and then, in one smooth movement, he set the plate and mug down on the counter and stepped toward her.

His hands were warm as they found her arms, anchoring her.

"Becky, breathe."

She hadn't even realized she was not.

His grip tightened—not forceful, just steady.

"I didn't want to wake you," he murmured. "I thought I'd make breakfast."

Something inside her cracked.

The fear, the panic—it released.

Becky let out a shaky, breathless laugh, pressing a hand to her forehead as the adrenaline slowly seeped out of her system.

"You scared the hell out of me."

Aaron's lips twitched.

"Sorry," he murmured. "Next time, I'll leave a note."

She let out another small laugh, but before she could pull away, he did something unexpected.

He pulled her in.

His arms wrapped around her, pulling her flush against his chest.

Becky melted into him instantly, pressing her face against his shirt, inhaling his warmth, his presence.

"I'm here," Aaron whispered against her hair. "I'm not going anywhere."

And finally, finally, she let herself believe it.

She was not alone.

Not anymore.

The Breakfast Catastrophe

The kitchen was bathed in morning light, golden beams cutting through the window, illuminating the dust motes that drifted lazily in the air. The faint hum of the refrigerator was the only sound at first, the silence between them stretching—not uncomfortable, but thick with something unspoken.

Becky wrapped her hands around the steaming mug of coffee Aaron had handed her, letting the warmth seep into her fingers. She hadn't realized how cold she was. Not just her skin, but something deeper—something buried inside of her, wound tight like a coil that had never truly loosened.

She stared down into the dark liquid, her reflection distorted by ripples of steam.

She still was not used to the quiet.

For days, her world had been filled with sound—the pounding of the rain, the wail of the wind, the distant hum of her own ragged breathing. And in the spaces between those noises, in the the suffocating stillness of her house, she had heard him.

Or maybe she had just heard herself.

The intrusive thoughts. The ones she couldn't shake.

The accident had stained her mind, seeping into every corner, every moment, refusing to let her breathe without feeling it lurking. The guilt, the terror, the gnawing certainty that she was not alone. That he had followed her. That she was being watched.

Even now, standing in the warmth of her kitchen, Aaron only inches away, she felt it. The residual unease, the weight of eyes that weren't there.

She blinked hard, trying to shake it off.

Not now. Not right now.

Aaron was watching her, his brows pinched together, that familiar concern etched into his features. He was not pushing, was not prying, but she knew that if she let herself slip too far, if she let the silence go on too long, he would notice. He always did.

Becky forced a small, breathless laugh as she pulled the coffee mug closer to her lips. "You cooked?" she murmured, her voice laced with equal parts surprise and apprehension.

Aaron smirked, leaning against the counter. "I attempted to," he corrected. "No promises on the quality."

Becky hesitated, inhaling the scent of the coffee, the rich bitterness curling into her lungs. It smelled... strong.

Too strong.

Like the coffee itself had been brewed with resentment and determination.

She took a sip.

A mistake.

The bitterness hit her tongue like a slap, coating her throat with an almost acidic intensity. She coughed, her face twisting, the warmth of the mug suddenly feeling less like comfort and more like a warning.

Aaron raised an eyebrow. "Well?"

Becky blinked at him, still swallowing the burn. She had to clear her throat before she could speak.

"Jesus, Aaron," she wheezed. "What the hell did you do to this?"

Aaron huffed, crossing his arms. "I made coffee."

"You made vengeful coffee," Becky muttered, setting the cup down cautiously, as if it might attack her. She swallowed again, still tasting whatever abomination he had created. "Did you just dump an entire bag of grounds in there and hope for the best?"

Aaron scowled. "I followed the instructions."

Becky gave him a pointed look. "Did you?"

Aaron hesitated, then glanced away. "...Kind of."

She snorted, shaking her head. "Okay. Let's try the food, then."

Aaron perked up slightly, stepping aside to let her see his masterpiece.

A plate sat in the center of the counter, a tower of pancakes stacked high, an attempt at breakfast glory.

But something was off.

The edges of the pancakes were dark—too dark—almost charred. And yet, the center still looked... undercooked. Somehow, he had managed to burn and undercook them at the same time.

Becky hesitated. Aaron noticed.

"They're fine," he said quickly, grabbing a fork and spearing one of the offending pancakes. The outer edge crunched. Loudly.

Becky frowned. "Is... is this made of adamantium?"

Aaron scowled. "Just eat it, Becky."

Becky pressed harder, applying actual force to the utensil. The outer edge finally gave way with a dramatic crunch, but as she pulled the piece apart, the center revealed itself—soft, sticky, very undercooked.

She looked at him, horrified. "Aaron. You have achieved the impossible."

Aaron blinked. "...What?"

"You have simultaneously burned and undercooked the same pancake."

Aaron exhaled, clearly questioning every life decision that had led him here. "Look, the first batch caught on fire—"

"Caught on fire?!" Becky's eyes widened.

"—so I tried turning the heat down," Aaron continued, ignoring her gasp. "Then I forgot to grease the pan, so I had to scrape those off. And then I might have flipped them too early. But they looked done."

Becky stared at him, then at the sad, defiant stack of pancakes on her plate. Then back at Aaron.

And then—despite herself—she burst out laughing.

It was not polite laughter. It was not a quiet giggle. It was real laughter, deep and sudden, shaking her shoulders, curling her forward as she clutched her stomach.

Aaron scowled. "Shut up."

"I can't!" Becky gasped between giggles. "What the hell happened here? Did you cook these over an open fire?"

Aaron sighed dramatically, rubbing his temples. "I forgot to grease the pan, okay? The first batch... didn't make it."

Becky wiped at her eyes. "So you incinerated the second?"

Aaron grumbled something under his breath, then grabbed a plate and handed it to her. "Just eat, before I regret trying."

Still grinning, Becky took her fork and hesitantly poked at the top pancake. The surface was rock solid.

She frowned. "Am I... am I supposed to cut this or file a police report for assault?"

Aaron threw his hands in the air. "Oh my God—just eat the damn pancake!"

Becky bit her lip to suppress another laugh before finally attempting to cut into it. The first press of her fork barely made a dent. The second required actual effort.

The third? The fork bent.

"Aaron." Becky stared at her now-warped utensil. "What did you put in these? Steel? Cement?"

Aaron dragged a hand down his face. "I do not know why I even try with you."

Becky finally took a bite.

It was bad.

Somehow, it was both dry and raw, like it couldn't decide what texture it wanted to be. The burned edges crumbled into dust in her mouth, but the center stuck to the roof of her mouth like sweet, sticky glue.

And yet—

She swallowed.

She forced herself to smile.

Because Aaron had tried.

And that meant something.

The simple fact that he was here, doing something ridiculous and unnecessary just to make her laugh, just to make her forget—even for a moment—meant everything.

Becky hesitated, lowering the fork as she stared at him.

He had always been there.

Long before any of this.

Through the dumb childhood fights, the teenage pranks, the late-night talks in high school when neither of them knew what the hell they were doing with their lives.

And now, he was here.

With inedible pancakes and awful coffee.

Because he didn't know how else to help.

Becky's smile softened.

Aaron watched her, his teasing smirk fading slightly, like he could feel the shift in the air between them.

He didn't say anything.

But he didn't have to.

For the first time in days, she felt safe.

Becky reached for the coffee again—grimacing immediately—but swallowed it down anyway.

Aaron chuckled, shaking his head. "you are really gonna drink that?"

Becky exhaled, setting the cup down with mock defeat. "Apparently, I'm into self-destruction."

Aaron smirked. "Noted."

She rolled her eyes.

But the warmth in her chest remained.

Maybe, just maybe—

She was not completely lost in the dark anymore.

She was not thinking about the accident.

She was not thinking about the man in the hoodie.

She was just here, laughing with Aaron, feeling lighter than she had in days.

And that—more than anything—was what mattered.

Aaron leaned against the counter, his smirk softening slightly. "You wanna go out today? Get some real food?"

Becky hesitated.

Going outside still felt wrong.

Unsafe.

But Aaron's eyes were steady, patient.

Waiting.

Finally, she exhaled.

"Fine," she muttered. "But if we go, I'm picking where."

Aaron grinned. "Sounds good."

Becky hesitated, stirring her coffee absentmindedly, the dark liquid swirling in slow circles. The thought of leaving—of stepping beyond the safety of these four walls—sent a cold trickle of uncertainty down her spine.

But then, a thought struck her.

She glanced up at Aaron, her lips twitching just slightly. "How about a nail salon?"

Aaron froze mid-sip, his brows pulling together in confusion. "A nail salon?"

Becky nodded, watching him closely, waiting for the inevitable reaction. "Yeah. I could get a manicure, and you"—her smirk deepened—"could get a pedicure."

Aaron stared at her, blinking slowly, like he was waiting for her to crack and admit she was joking.

She didn't.

His mouth parted slightly, a mixture of mild horror and amusement flickering across his face. "You want me—me—to go get my nails done?"

Becky shrugged, taking a deliberate sip of her coffee. "Why not? I mean, you did just say you wanted to go anywhere."

Aaron narrowed his eyes, suspicious. "You just want to see me suffer."

Becky's smirk widened. "Maybe."

A short silence stretched between them, and then Aaron let out a dramatic sigh, running a hand through his hair. "Alright. Fine. But if I'm doing this, I get to pick lunch afterward."

Becky tilted her head. "Deal. But—" she leaned in slightly, lowering her voice just enough to make it sound conspiratorial, "—if you are getting a pedicure, I get to pick the color."

Aaron groaned, already regretting every decision that had led him to this moment. "Jesus, Beck."

Becky simply arched an eyebrow, her grin growing. "Chicken?"

Aaron leaned forward, resting his forearms against the table, his smirk returning despite himself. "Oh, I'll do it," he said, his voice rich with challenge. "But if you pick some neon pink or glittery disaster, I'm making you wear matching socks for a week."

Becky pretended to consider it, then grinned. "Worth it."

Aaron shook his head, muttering something under his breath, but there was something lighter in his expression now, something that hadn't been there before.

And for the first time in days, Becky felt a little bit like herself again.

CHAPTER NINE

Painted Nails & Unseen Shadows

A Shadow Between Us

The rhythmic hum of the tires against the wet pavement filled the car, a steady, hypnotic sound that blurred the edges of reality. It was the kind of white noise that could lull someone into a false sense of peace—the soft, ceaseless vibration of movement, the gentle sway of the vehicle as it rolled over scattered debris. A metronome marking the passage of time.

Outside, the world wore its wounds openly. The storm had passed, but its aftermath lingered—tree limbs broken and twisted like discarded bones, rainwater pooling in the dips of uneven pavement, leaves plastered against windshields and sidewalks in sodden, clinging masses. Some houses bore fresh blue tarps hastily stretched over gaping wounds in their roofs, the color jarring against the muted gray sky. Everything felt unsettled. Recovering, but not yet healed.

Becky stared out the window, her breath ghosting against the cool glass, creating a foggy halo that blurred the already smudged world beyond. She watched it all—the evidence of chaos, the way the earth seemed to sigh in exhaustion beneath the weight of the storm's fury—but it felt distant. Like something happening to someone else. A film she was watching through thick, distorting glass. Detached.

She let her eyelids drift shut, the pull of exhaustion dragging at her limbs like unseen hands. It was not the kind of tiredness that could be fixed with a good night's sleep. No, this was deeper. A weariness that had embedded itself into her bones, woven itself into the very fabric of her being. The past few days had drained her, leaving her feeling hollow, like a marionette with cut strings. Her body craved rest, but her mind... her mind refused to grant it.

Aaron glanced over at her, his grip tightening slightly on the wheel as he took her in—the way her shoulders had finally eased, the lines of tension that had carved themselves into her face smoothing out in slumber. She looked different like this. Softer. Unburdened, if only temporarily.

For the first time in days, she looked... at peace.

His lips twitched into something that almost resembled a smile, the sight of her like a balm against the constant undercurrent of worry that had been gnawing at his chest. It was fleeting, but it was there. A fragile moment of calm in the storm that had become their lives.

And then, in an instant, that peace shattered.

Aaron inhaled sharply, his fingers stiffening against the leather-wrapped steering wheel.

Something was not right.

At the corner ahead, beneath the skeletal reach of an old oak tree, a figure stood.

The hood was up. The face was obscured. But Aaron felt him.

The weight of his gaze was like ice sliding down his spine, an oppressive, suffocating presence that coiled around his chest like a vise. Cold. Unrelenting. Watching.

His heartbeat pounded in his ears, a deep, foreboding pulse that sent adrenaline spiking through his system. Every nerve in his body screamed at him to do something—to turn the car around, to confront, to flee. But he couldn't move. He could only stare, his breath shallow, his fingers tightening so hard around the wheel that his knuckles turned white.

The figure didn't move.

Didn't shift.

Didn't blink.

Aaron forced himself to check the road, his vision tunneling, his hands slick against the wheel as he took a breath, trying to ground himself. Trying to think. He looked back—

Gone.

His stomach twisted violently. His pulse spiked, erratic, the air in the car suddenly feeling too thick, too close. His grip faltered for just a second before he pressed down on the gas pedal a little harder than necessary, his body tense, wired, desperate to put distance between them.

He flicked a quick glance at Becky, his chest tightening when he saw she hadn't stirred. She was still curled against the window, her head tilted just slightly, lips parted in the smallest of exhales. Peaceful.

She hadn't seen him.

Thank God.

Shadows in the Glass

As Aaron pulled into the parking lot, his eyes darted sharply, scanning the pavement, the sidewalk, the shifting shadows stretching along the storefronts.

Looking for him.

The lot was not busy—only a handful of cars scattered throughout, their rain-speckled surfaces reflecting the dull gray of the sky. A light breeze rustled through the air, carrying the faint scent of wet pavement and something distant—something cold.

Aaron's grip on the steering wheel tightened before he forced himself to let go. Breathe. His knuckles ached from how hard he had been clenching.

He exhaled slowly, turning his head just enough to steal a glance at Becky.

She hadn't noticed.

Her hands were fidgeting slightly, fingers tapping against her knee in a quiet rhythm, but her face remained neutral. Maybe even... calm. The heaviness she had carried for days seemed to sit a little lighter on her shoulders.

Aaron wanted to keep it that way.

So when they both climbed out of the car and headed toward the nail salon's entrance, he kept his steps even, his posture casual, all while his eyes flickered over every possible hiding spot.

Watching.

Waiting.

Hoping Becky didn't notice.

The bell above the salon door chimed softly as they stepped inside, the artificial warmth wrapping around them like a stark contrast to the outside air.

The scent of acetone and lavender curled through the space, mingling with the low murmur of conversation, the quiet hum of pedicure chairs whirring to life. It was bright inside—too bright—fluorescent lights washing over every polished surface, bouncing off the glossy countertops and neatly arranged rows of nail polish bottles in every imaginable shade.

It was the kind of place where nothing bad was supposed to happen.

Becky stepped forward, immediately drawn to the display of color swatches on the counter, flipping through them with a look of serious consideration, like she was solving a mystery rather than picking a nail color.

Aaron hovered near the waiting area, his gaze lingering on her.

She looked lighter.

Not completely back to herself—not yet. But there was something about the way she stood, the way her shoulders had loosened, the way she debated between two nearly identical shades of purple with an expression of deep internal struggle, that made him exhale some of the tension that had been strangling him since that night.

She needed this.

And maybe, Aaron realized, so did he.

For the first time in days, the weight pressing against his chest lifted just enough for him to breathe.

Then something shifted.

A flicker of movement.

Aaron's entire body locked up. His breath stalled. The tight coil of unease that had loosened a second ago snapped back into place like a steel trap.

His eyes snapped to the window.

The large front pane of glass stretched from floor to ceiling, showcasing the lot outside. Sunlight streaked across it, creating a harsh glare, making it difficult to see beyond the reflection of the bright interior.

But through the glare—

A figure.

Aaron's stomach dropped.

Him.

The man in the gray hoodie stood just outside. Still. Unmoving.

Aaron's lungs seized.

The hood was drawn up, obscuring his face, but it didn't matter. Aaron felt his stare. Sharp. Piercing. Wrong. A gaze that crawled under his skin, digging in like cold fingers wrapping around his ribs.

Watching.

Aaron's fingers dug into his thighs, his pulse hammering violently against his ribs. The urge to move—to do something, anything—was instant and overwhelming. His body screamed at him to go outside, to confront him, to end this sick game once and for all.

But something held him back.

Instinct.

Becky.

He needed to think. He needed to be smart.

His gaze snapped to her, his heart slamming against his ribs.

Please do not look. Please do not see him.

She was still turned away, chatting with the technician, blissfully unaware of the shadow lurking just beyond the glass. Her lips curled into something resembling a smile as she pointed at one of the colors. Normal. Relaxed. Safe.

The moment was so painfully delicate, so impossibly normal, that Aaron felt a visceral, all-consuming need to protect it.

To protect her.

Aaron's hands curled into tighter fists, his nails biting into his palms as he forced himself to breathe through the terror clawing at his throat.

Then—

He blinked.

Gone.

Again.

Aaron's breath hitched sharply, his muscles still coiled, his eyes darting frantically back to where the man had been.

The spot was empty.

The sidewalk stretched before him, undisturbed. No movement. No trace.

Nothing.

Aaron's jaw tightened, a sharp pulse of frustration and dread crashing through him. His breath came out in short, steady bursts, the fight-or-flight instinct still thrumming beneath his skin.

Had he imagined it?

No.

It was real. Just like at the stop sign.

But if it was real, then how the hell did he keep disappearing?

Aaron swallowed hard, forcing himself to loosen his grip, to push down the panic threatening to drag him under. He couldn't afford to spiral.

Not here.

Not now.

Not when Becky was finally breathing again.

He let out a slow, measured breath, stealing one last glance at her.

She was still lost in the trivial struggle of picking a shade of purple, her brow furrowed in over-exaggerated concentration as if this were the most important decision she had ever made in her life.

She had no idea what had just happened.

And for now—

That was a mercy.

Aaron shifted his focus back to the window.

The sun's glare distorted everything beyond the glass, stretching the light in odd angles, obscuring the edges of the world outside.

But deep down, in the part of him that knew better—

He felt it.

The eyes were still there.

Watching.

A Splash of Color in the Dark

Becky sat cross-legged in the plush pedicure chair, the gentle whir of the massage feature vibrating beneath her, as she held up two small bottles of nail polish, wiggling them teasingly in front of Aaron's face.

"All right, big guy. Which one are you going with?"

The bottles clinked softly as she tilted them from side to side, the light catching on the glossy glass, illuminating the two shades of purple—one soft and delicate like spring lilacs, the other deep and rich, almost royal.

Aaron, seated in the chair beside her, stretched out his legs in the warm foot bath, feigning deep contemplation. He rubbed his chin as if this were a decision of great importance, his brows furrowing in an exaggerated display of seriousness.

"Hmm," he mused, his voice low and thoughtful. "Purple."

Becky arched an eyebrow. "Seriously? you are going with purple?"

His lips twitched into a smirk, the faintest ghost of amusement flickering behind his eyes.

"It's your favorite color, isn't it?"

Becky stilled.

Her fingers tightened slightly around the small glass bottles, her teasing expression faltering for just a second.

Something in the air shifted.

For a moment, she just stared at him—really stared—like she was not sure whether to laugh or cry. Like his words had hit something deeper than either of them expected.

The weight of them settled between them, soft but heavy, pressing against something fragile inside her.

Finally, she swallowed, her voice quieter when she murmured, "Yeah. It is."

The silence that followed was thick, but not uncomfortable. It stretched between them, warm and unspoken, filled with the things neither of them knew how to put into words.

Thank you.

I see you.

I know you.

Even when you feel like you are fading, I still see you.

But neither of them said any of that.

Instead, they let the moment settle, let it breathe.

They sat side by side, feet soaking in warm water, the slow curl of lavender-scented steam drifting between them. The tension that had been wrapped around Becky for days had loosened, her body melting into the chair in a way Aaron hadn't seen in... too long.

She was relaxed.

And for the first time in what felt like forever, so was he.

The nail technician hummed softly as she reached for the bottle Aaron had chosen—the boldest, most obnoxiously vibrant shade of purple available—and twisted the cap open with an audible *pop*.

Aaron glanced sideways, catching the glint of mischief in Becky's eye as she bit back a smirk.

"You know," she mused, her voice slow, teasing, "I thought you were going to chicken out."

Aaron huffed. "Please. I do not back down from a challenge."

Becky smirked. "Oh, really?"

"I've survived our friendship this long, haven't I?"

She snorted. "Barely."

He grinned, shaking his head as he settled deeper into his chair, watching as the brush stroked across his toenails, painting them one by one in that ridiculously bright purple.

When Becky's nails were painted a soft lavender, delicate and effortless, and Aaron's toes were a vibrant, unholy shade of royal violet, Becky looked down at them—at their feet, side by side, matching in some ridiculous, unexpected way—and...

She laughed.

A real, genuine laugh.

Not forced. Not hesitant. Not the kind of brittle, hollow sound she had used to cover the cracks in her voice for days.

Just Becky.

Alive. Bright. Unburdened.

Aaron turned his head slightly, watching her as the sound filled the space, warm and weightless, lifting something inside him that had been sinking for far too long.

And in that moment—he knew.

He would do anything to keep that sound from fading again.

A Shadow in the Parking Lot

The scent of lavender oil and acetone still clung to the air as Becky and Aaron stepped out of the nail salon and into the crisp evening. The storm had passed, but the air still carried its bite—a sharp chill that nipped at exposed skin, whispering of the cold that lingered in its wake. The pavement glistened under the dull glow of streetlights, still slick with the remnants of the rain, puddles reflecting distorted patches of neon from the nearby storefront signs.

Becky crossed her arms loosely over her chest, rubbing her hands along her bare skin to chase away the cold. But inside, she felt warm. Lighter.

For the first time in what felt like ages, she felt like herself again.

She glanced down at her freshly painted toes, the deep royal purple peeking through her sandals. It was a small thing, almost ridiculous, but it grounded her. It reminded her of the laughter, the teasing, the gentle banter that had passed between her and Aaron just moments ago. It reminded her that there was still room for something other than fear.

She looked over at Aaron. His hands were tucked into his jacket pockets, but there was a casual ease to his posture that hadn't been there before. He seemed more relaxed—his usual confidence settling back into place, like he was not carrying all of her weight alongside his own anymore.

She almost smiled.

And then—

It happened.

The feeling.

It slammed into her so suddenly that it was like being doused in ice water.

Her breath caught. Her body locked up.

The world around her slowed, the background noise of the parking lot fading into a dull, distant hum. Her stomach twisted violently, a primal instinct flaring deep inside her—something was wrong.

Aaron stiffened beside her, his entire frame going rigid.

He didn't need to follow her gaze to know what she saw. He already felt it.

That presence. That stare.

Aaron's jaw tightened, his teeth grinding together as his eyes flicked toward the far end of the lot.

And there he was.

The man in the gray hoodie.

Standing motionless beside a parked car, half-shrouded in shadows.

Just like before.

Watching.

Aaron inhaled sharply, his breath flaring in his nostrils, and rage flared in his chest like a match igniting gasoline.

"He's fucking back again." His voice low and sharp, a blade honed to a dangerous edge.

Becky's head snapped toward him, panic slicing through her like a knife. "What?" Her voice cracked, raw and unfiltered. "**What do you mean 'back again'? You've seen him before?"

Aaron hesitated. Just for a second.

"Twice today," he admitted, his voice tight and clipped. "At the stop sign. And again outside the salon while you were picking your nail color."

Becky felt the world tilt slightly beneath her feet. Her vision blurred at the edges, her heartbeat hammered a violent, unsteady rhythm.

Her fingers curled around the strap of her purse, gripping it so tightly her knuckles ached. "Aaron, what if it's—" She swallowed hard, forcing air into her lungs. The words felt too big, too heavy.

Her throat locked up, her voice breaking.

"What if it's the man I...?"

She couldn't finish.

Aaron turned toward her so fast that she barely registered the movement before his hands were gripping her shoulders—firm, steady, and grounding.

"Hey." His voice was low and controlled, but there was no mistaking the urgency in it. His eyes locked onto hers, dark and unwavering. "It's okay. We'll figure this out. But right now, we need to get home."

Becky forced a shaky breath past her lips, trying to tether herself to the steadiness of his voice.

The weight of his hands. The warmth of his skin.

After a moment, she nodded.

Aaron lingered just long enough to make sure she was not going to fall apart, then slowly released her.

And then he turned back.

The man in the hoodie hadn't moved.

Still standing there.

Still watching.

Aaron's blood boiled.

Every muscle in his body coiled with tension, his hands clenching into fists at his sides. He wanted to march across the parking lot and rip that fucking hood off, to see the face behind those cold, unrelenting eyes.

But something held him back.

The way the figure stood so still.

So completely, eerily motionless.

Aaron took a step forward—

A car passed.

Headlights flashed, sweeping across the lot—

And then, just like that—

Gone.

Like a shadow swallowed by the dark.

Aaron's breath came out in short, furious bursts. His pulse pounded in his skull, rage mixing with something he refused to name.

Fucking coward.

With one last glare at the empty space where the man had stood, Aaron turned back, yanked the car door open, and growled, "Let's go."

The Ride Home: A Silence Too Loud

The drive home was heavy—thick with something unspoken, something suffocating. The quiet was not comforting. It was oppressive, pressing against Becky's chest like a weight she couldn't shake.

She sat rigid in her seat, her fingers twisting restlessly in her lap. Every few seconds, her eyes flickered toward the passenger-side window, scanning the blurred scenery beyond. Searching. Expecting.

She didn't know what terrified her more—the idea of seeing him again or the possibility that she would not.

The rhythmic hum of the tires on wet pavement should have been soothing, should have pulled her into that dazed state that always came after exhaustion had wrung her dry. But her body refused to relax, her nerves wound too tight, her mind replaying the moment outside the nail salon over and over again.

Aaron hadn't said much since they got into the car. She could feel his tension—see it in the way his hands gripped the wheel too tightly, his knuckles paling from the force. His jaw was set, his muscles coiled like he was ready to strike at any moment.

Like he was waiting.

Neither of them acknowledged the fact that she hadn't stopped trembling.

She bit her lip, staring out into the darkness beyond the glass. "Do you think he'll follow us?"

Aaron inhaled sharply, but he didn't look at her. His focus stayed on the road, his fingers flexing around the wheel. "I do not know." His voice was tight, controlled, like he was holding something back. "But if he does, I swear to God, Becky, I'll—"

He cut himself off.

She turned toward him, studying his profile in the dim glow of the dashboard lights. His jaw was clenched so tight she thought he might crack a tooth. The muscle there ticked, his breaths coming slower, deeper, measured—like he was trying to stop himself from saying something he'd regret.

Or something he couldn't take back.

Becky exhaled through her nose and looked down at her hands. They were still curled into tight fists against her lap. She forced them open, flexing her fingers, trying to shake off the lingering chill in her bones.

She hated this.

She hated feeling helpless. Hated that Aaron had to be on edge because of her. Hated that no matter what she did—no matter how much she wanted to move past it—the shadow of that night still would not let her go.

Would it ever?

Aaron suddenly pulled into a parking lot, easing the car into a space outside a small restaurant. Becky blinked at him, startled.

"What are we doing?" she asked, her voice quieter than she intended.

Aaron finally turned to look at her, and something in his expression softened. Just a little. "Getting food." He nodded toward the neon sign that flickered lazily above the entrance. "You need to eat."

Becky frowned, her stomach twisting—not from hunger, but from the thought of forcing something down when her insides already felt knotted. "Aaron, I—"

"No arguments," he interrupted gently. "you are barely holding it together as it is. I can hear your stomach growling from here."

She opened her mouth to protest, but the look in his eyes made the words die in her throat.

She didn't realize how badly she needed him to take control of something—anything—until he did.

So, she just sighed and unbuckled her seatbelt.

Inside the small pizza place, the warmth should have been inviting, but Becky felt exposed. The walls were lined with wide windows, reflections bouncing off the glass, making it impossible to tell if someone was looking in—or if it was just the ghosts in her head playing tricks on her.

Aaron stood close. Too close. His arm brushed hers every time they moved, his presence grounding but also buzzing with restless energy.

She could tell he felt it too.

That wrongness. That feeling like something was just out of sight.

They barely spoke as they waited. Becky's arms stayed crossed tightly over her chest, her fingers gripping her own skin like an anchor. The overhead lights buzzed, the low murmur of other diners blending into background noise she couldn't quite focus on.

When their order was ready, Aaron took the box without a word, leading her back to the car with the same tense posture he'd worn all day.

Neither of them exhaled until the doors shut behind them.

A Desperate Idea

The drive home was shorter than Becky expected.

Or maybe she had just lost track of time.

Aaron parked in the driveway, letting the car idle for a moment before finally shifting into park. He didn't move right away. Neither did she.

The silence stretched between them again.

Then, without looking at her, he said, "We need help."

Becky's brows furrowed as she turned toward him, the shift in his tone sending an uneasy chill through her. "What are you saying?"

Aaron finally dragged a hand down his face, exhaling through gritted teeth. "I mean, I do not know what the hell is going on, Beck. I do not know why this guy keeps showing up or if it's all in our heads or if—" He stopped himself, shaking his head. "I do not know. But we need to do something. We can't just sit here and wait for him to show up again."

Becky swallowed hard. She agreed. God, she agreed.

But what could they do?

She was still struggling to answer that when Aaron spoke again.

"My aunt," he said slowly, like he was not sure he wanted to say it out loud, "used to rave about this psychic she went to. Swore up and down the woman was the real deal."

Becky blinked at him, surprised. "A psychic?"

Aaron sighed, rubbing the back of his neck. "I know how it sounds, but—"

"No, I mean..." Becky trailed off, thinking. Was it really that crazy? After everything that had happened—after seeing that hooded figure appear and vanish, after feeling those eyes where they shouldn't be—could she really say a psychic was any less believable than anything else?

Her fingers curled against her thighs. "You think she could help?"

Aaron looked at her, his dark eyes searching. "I do not know. But I think it's worth a shot."

Becky hesitated, chewing the inside of her cheek. It still felt ridiculous. But then again... so did all of this.

She exhaled shakily. "Okay," she murmured finally. "We'll try it."

Relief flickered across Aaron's face, so brief she almost missed it. He nodded. "We'll call her tomorrow."

And just like that, the decision was made.

Neither of them knew what to expect.

Neither of them knew if it would change anything.

But at least now, they had a direction.

And that was better than nothing.

The Meal the Never Was

The house was quiet as they stepped inside, the air thick with the scent of warm pizza. It should have been comforting—familiar—but it was not. Not tonight.

Aaron set the pizza box on the counter with a dull thud, the sound too loud in the stillness. Becky hovered near the doorway, arms wrapped around herself, staring at it as if the mere thought of eating was too much.

Aaron moved without a word, heading toward the cabinet to grab some plates. The routine was almost automatic—something normal, something simple, something that should have been easy. But as he placed the plates down, he hesitated.

Neither of them moved to open the box right away.

After a long beat, Becky reached forward, flipping it open with a sigh. The smell of melted cheese and grease filled the space, but it didn't stir her hunger. Didn't stir anything.

Aaron grabbed a slice first, not because he wanted it, but because he felt like he should. Becky did the same, their movements slow, robotic, like they were just going through the motions.

They sat down at the table, the pizza in their hands, but neither took a bite.

Aaron stared down at his slice, barely seeing it. His mind was somewhere else—everywhere else. The psychic. The hooded figure. Becky's face when she asked if it was him—the man from the accident.

He couldn't shake the image.

Beside him, Becky was not faring much better. She held her slice, turning it slightly, studying the uneven strings of cheese stretching toward the crust. She swallowed hard, but not from hunger.

There were too many thoughts. Too many emotions knotted up inside her.

She could feel Aaron next to her, just as still, just as lost in the weight of it all.

A minute passed. Maybe more.

Finally, she exhaled and set her slice back in the box.

Aaron followed, pushing his plate away.

They didn't say anything. Didn't need to.

Without discussion, they both stood, their bodies moving in sync toward the bedroom, drawn by the only comfort they had left—each other.

The Weight of Sleep

The bedroom was dim, the soft glow from the bedside lamp casting faint, golden shadows across the walls. Neither of them spoke as they climbed into bed, settling into the silence like it was the only language they understood.

Becky curled into Aaron's side, resting her head against his chest. His warmth was immediate, seeping into her skin, wrapping around her like a shield against everything lurking in the darkness.

She listened to the steady rhythm of his breathing, the way his chest rose and fell beneath her. Slow. Deep. Safe.

Aaron draped an arm around her, pulling her closer, his fingers absently tracing slow, comforting circles against her back. The gesture was simple, instinctive, but it was enough.

Neither of them spoke about the fear still gripping them.

Neither of them spoke about the psychic.

Neither of them spoke about him.

The silence stretched, not empty, but full. Full of thoughts, of unspoken worries, of things they were too exhausted to voice.

Becky felt the tension in Aaron's body slowly ease as sleep began to take him, his breaths growing heavier, his hold around her slackening slightly—but never fully letting go.

She let her eyes close, focusing on the sound of him. The way he breathed. The warmth of his skin. The solid, steady presence of him beside her.

For the first time all night, the fear didn't feel quite so suffocating.

And then, finally—mercifully—sleep came for her too.

CHAPTER TEN

A Visitor in the Dark

The pizza sat abandoned on the counter, its greasy aroma hanging thick in the air, untouched and forgotten. The box remained open, slices left untouched, a silent testament to their unsettled minds. Hours ago, they had brought it home, intending to eat, but neither had been able to stomach more than a bite. Now, it sat there, growing cold beneath the dull glow of the kitchen light, just another thing overshadowed by the weight of the night.

In the bedroom, Becky lay curled against Aaron, her head resting against his chest, her body molded against his warmth. His arm was wrapped securely around her, his grip firm, grounding. The steady rise and fall of his breathing beneath her cheek lulled her into something resembling peace. Not quite sleep—never truly restful—but a fragile moment of quiet.

Then—

A thump.

Becky's body jolted awake, her breath hitching as her eyes snapped open. The sound had been low, deep—too deliberate to be the house settling, too heavy to be the wind rattling against the window.

Her fingers instinctively tightened against Aaron's ribs.

"Did you hear that?" she whispered, barely able to force the words out.

Aaron stirred beneath her, inhaling sharply as sleep slipped from his grasp. His body went rigid beneath hers, every muscle tensing as he listened.

Then, after a second—another thump.

His grip on her shifted. "Yeah," he murmured, voice husky with sleep but edged with something sharper, something alert.

Becky swallowed hard as Aaron gently lifted her off of him, shifting her aside as he sat up. The warmth of his body left her, and suddenly the bed felt colder, the air around them heavier.

"Stay here," he instructed, voice low, steady.

Her breath trembled. "Aaron—"

"I'll check it out."

She watched as he swung his legs over the side of the bed and stood, his movements careful, quiet. The room felt too dark now, the shadows stretching in unnatural ways.

Becky clutched the blanket tighter around her shoulders, shrinking into herself as Aaron stepped toward the doorway.

The moment he left the room, the air changed.

Something in the Dark

The house felt different.

Aaron could feel it in the way the air pressed against his skin—thick, suffocating, wrong.

He moved cautiously, his bare feet soundless against the floor. The hallway stretched out before him, bathed in slivers of moonlight filtering through the windows. Every shadow felt deeper, every darkened corner held the promise of something unseen.

His pulse pounded in his ears, his breath slow and controlled as he moved toward the source of the noise.

The living room lay ahead, dimly lit by the distant streetlamp outside. The furniture cast long, distorted shadows against the walls. The faint hum of the refrigerator droned on in the background, the only sign of normalcy in an otherwise unnatural stillness.

Then—

Aaron froze.

A figure stood in the far corner.

Still. Unmoving.

Watching.

The man in the gray hoodie.

Aaron's breath caught in his throat, his entire body locking up in an instant. The figure was nestled in the darkest part of the room, barely visible, but there was no mistaking him.

The hood was pulled low over his face, concealing his features, but Aaron could feel his gaze.

Cold. Unrelenting.

His fingers curled into fists at his sides, a slow, burning rage creeping into his veins, battling the ice-cold fear settling deep in his gut.

"Who the hell are you?" His voice was low, controlled, but it carried an edge of restrained fury.

The figure didn't move.

Didn't speak.

Didn't breathe.

Aaron's pulse pounded, his heart a violent drumbeat against his ribs. His instincts screamed at him—this isn't normal. This isn't a man.

Aaron took a slow, deliberate step forward. "What do you want?" His voice cut through the silence like a blade.

Still—nothing.

The man didn't flinch. Didn't acknowledge him. Just watched.

Aaron's jaw tightened, every muscle coiled with adrenaline, ready for a fight. His breath came in slow, even exhales, his body wound so tight he thought he might snap.

Then—

The lights flickered.

A sharp pulse of darkness swallowed the room, just for a breath, just for the span of a blink—

And when the light returned—

Gone.

Aaron's breath left him in a ragged exhale.

The air instantly felt lighter.

But he didn't.

His skin crawled with the ghost of something unseen, his nerves still wired, his body still on edge.

He swept his gaze around the room, scanning every shadow, every doorway, searching. But the presence was gone. The space where the figure had stood was empty.

But Aaron knew—he had been there.

He had felt it.

This was not just paranoia. This was real.

Aaron backed out of the room slowly, his senses still on high alert. His body vibrated with unease, his fists still clenched, his breath coming in measured inhales.

With one last scan of the living room, he turned and made his way back down the hall, his steps quicker this time, more urgent.

When he reached the bedroom, Becky was already sitting up, her body stiff, her eyes wide and searching.

The second he stepped inside, she bolted upright.

"What was it?"

Aaron hesitated.

He could lie.

Tell her it was nothing.

But the fear in her eyes, the way she gripped the blanket so tight her knuckles turned white—he couldn't.

He exhaled slowly. "I saw him." His voice was rough, quieter than he expected. "The man in the gray hoodie. He was standing in the living room."

Becky's breath hitched. Her fingers trembled.

"He was here?" Her voice was barely above a whisper, thick with something broken, something raw.

Aaron nodded, moving to sit beside her. He dragged a hand down his face, feeling the exhaustion settle deep in his bones. "Yeah. But he's gone now." His words didn't even sound convincing to himself. "I do not know how, but... he's gone."

Becky shook her head, her whole body trembling now.

"He's not gone, Aaron. He's never gone. He's always there. Waiting."

Her voice cracked, and suddenly, all the strength drained from her body. She folded inward, her arms wrapping around herself as if she could physically hold herself together.

Aaron didn't hesitate.

He reached for her, pulling her into his arms, holding her against him. She melted into his chest, fingers fisting the fabric of his shirt, her breath uneven, shaky.

"I'm not going to let him hurt you," he murmured against her hair, his voice steady, firm. Certain. "I'll stay right here. you are safe with me."

She didn't respond.

She just buried herself deeper into him, her breath warm against his skin, her body trembling in his hold.

Aaron didn't sleep that night.

His gaze remained fixed on the doorway.

Watching.

Waiting.

Because deep down, he knew—

This was not over.

CHAPTER ELEVEN

A Taste of Something Real

A Restless Night, A Heavy Heart

Aaron never slept.

The hours stretched long and restless, pressing down on him with a weight that refused to lift. He lay still, his gaze locked on the faint slivers of light creeping through the blinds, his mind a relentless storm of unease. The house was silent—too silent. The kind of quiet that was not peaceful but hollow, stretched tight like a wire about to snap.

Every time he closed his eyes, the images resurfaced.

The hooded figure.

Standing in the corner.

Watching.

Waiting.

Then—gone.

But it was not over.

Aaron *knew* it was not over.

His arm remained wrapped around Becky, her small frame curled against him, her warmth bleeding into him. He held her close, as if his grip alone could keep her safe, could shield her from the presence that lurked just beyond reason. Her breath was soft and steady, the slow rise and fall of her chest the only indication that she had, somehow, managed to find rest.

He envied that.

The ability to shut it all out—even if only for a few hours.

His own exhaustion was bone-deep, clinging to his limbs like lead, but sleep would not come. It refused. His body felt drained, but his mind remained sharp, spinning with the same relentless thoughts, the same silent anxieties gnawing at his gut.

He was not sure how long he lay like that, rigid and alert, his ears straining for any sound beyond their quiet breaths. The minutes blurred together, then the hours. At some point, the deep black of the room began to shift, fading into the pale blue-gray of early morning.

Then Becky stirred.

She shifted slightly against him, her breath catching as she blinked awake, her eyelashes fluttering against his skin. For a brief moment, she looked disoriented—her body tensed slightly, her fingers twitching where they rested against his chest. Her eyes flickered around the room, searching, cautious.

Then she found him.

The tension in her frame eased instantly, her shoulders relaxing as recognition softened her features. The corner of her lips lifted into a fragile, sleepy smile.

"Morning," she murmured, her voice thick with sleep, warm and slow.

Aaron forced a small smile in return, though the exhaustion carved into his bones made it feel heavier than usual. "Morning."

She stretched, a lazy, languid motion, her fingertips grazing his bare chest. A quiet sigh slipped from her lips—content yet disbelieving.

"I actually slept," she admitted, like she didn't quite believe it herself. Then, softer, "Thanks to you."

Aaron let out a breathy chuckle, though it carried a weight he didn't bother to hide. "Happy to help."

Becky propped herself up slightly, brushing tangled strands of hair from her face as she peered down at him. The movement exposed more of her bare shoulder, her skin dappled in the soft morning light filtering through the window. She studied him for a long moment, something flickering in her gaze—something hesitant, unspoken.

Then she spoke.

"Hey, I was thinking... maybe we should both take a shower before we head out."

Aaron arched a brow, smirking faintly. "Sounds good. You go first, though. Save me some hot water."

She rolled her eyes, but there was something else beneath the amusement—something quieter. A small shift. A quiet pause.

Her fingers traced absent patterns against the sheets, the nervous energy betraying the casual tone she was trying to maintain.

"Well..." she started, softer now. "I was thinking... maybe we both shower."

Aaron blinked.

His smirk faltered—not from discomfort, but from surprise. He hadn't expected that.

"Like, together?" he asked, brow lifting slightly.

Becky's cheeks warmed just a little, but she didn't look away. She held his gaze, something raw and open in her eyes.

"Yeah," she admitted. Her voice was playful, but there was a vulnerability beneath it, something more fragile than she wanted to let on. "I mean... we already slept together. What's the big deal?" She tried to make it sound light, casual, but then she exhaled, her fingers curling slightly in the sheets.

"And... I just do not want to be alone right now."

Aaron's chest tightened.

That was it. That was the real reason.

She didn't have to say more.

He understood.

He saw it in the way she chewed her lip, in the way her fingers would not stay still, in the way her body had instinctively curled closer to his as she spoke, like she was afraid of the space between them.

The night hadn't erased anything.

Not the fear.

Not the weight pressing on her.

She was still carrying it.

But she didn't want to carry it alone.

Aaron reached up, brushing his knuckles gently along her jaw, tilting her chin just enough so he could see her clearly.

"Alright," he murmured, offering her a soft, reassuring smile.

"Let's do it."

Relief flickered in her eyes, quick and subtle, but it was there.

She nodded once, then slid out from beneath the covers, moving toward the bathroom without another word.

Aaron followed.

And as the warm steam began to curl around them, the outside world—the fear, the exhaustion, the unknown—faded into the background, if only for a little while.

A Fragile Moment in the Steam

The bathroom filled quickly with the sound of rushing water, a steady cascade that blurred the edges of the world beyond the door. Steam curled in thick ribbons, wrapping around the mirror, swallowing the space in warmth. The scent of lavender and soap coated the air, clinging to their skin before they even stepped in.

Becky stepped in first, her breath hitching slightly as the hot water crashed over her bare shoulders, rolling in rivulets down her spine. She tilted her head back, closing her eyes, letting the warmth sink deep into her muscles, easing the tension that had been wound so tightly inside her for days.

A sigh slipped from her lips—soft, relieved.

Aaron followed, stepping in behind her.

The space around them shrank instantly.

The shower was not small, but the heat, the closeness, the absence of anything between them made every movement careful, hesitant.

For the first few moments, it was awkward—their bodies brushing as they adjusted, both of them unsure where to put their hands, their elbows knocking together in the confined space. Aaron reached for the soap at the same time Becky moved to rinse her hair, and their arms tangled for a fumbling moment.

Becky turned, amusement flickering in her expression.

"Relax, Aaron," she murmured, lips curving. "It's just me."

Aaron huffed a quiet laugh, raking a hand through his wet hair. "You say that like I'm nervous."

"Aren't you?" she teased, voice light, though there was something more in her eyes—something knowing.

He hesitated.

Then exhaled.

"Maybe a little," he admitted. "But not in a bad way."

She stepped closer, closing the remaining space between them, the warm water trailing down the curve of her collarbone, between them, where their bodies hovered just shy of touching. Her hands lifted, pressing lightly against his chest, fingers tracing absent shapes along his skin.

"You do not have to be nervous around me," she murmured, her voice soft, certain. "It's just us."

Aaron let out a slow breath, his hands finally settling on her waist, his thumbs brushing against her damp skin. "I know."

For a moment, they simply stood there, wrapped in the hum of water and the weight of something unspoken.

Becky leaned up, pressing a kiss to his lips—soft, slow, not like the night before.

This was not heat.

was not urgency.

It was something else entirely.

Something deeper.

Something steady.

A reminder that no matter what shadows loomed outside, they were here.

Together.

Aaron kissed her back, just as slow, just as lingering, anchoring himself in that moment, in *her*. His fingers splayed across the small of her back, tracing circles against her skin, pulling her just a little closer.

Becky melted into him, her body molding against his, her hands sliding up, over his shoulders, curling into the damp strands of his hair.

For the first time in days, she felt safe.

Not because the fear was gone. Not because the nightmare was over.

But because *he* was here.

And right now, that was enough.

Fleeting Moments of Normalcy

By the time they stepped out of the shower, the air was thick with steam, swirling in dense clouds that clung to the mirrors and softened the edges of the room. The warmth of it still wrapped around them, but already, the air beyond the bathroom felt colder, heavier.

Becky reached for a towel, securing it tightly around herself before tossing another toward Aaron. He caught it with one hand, running the fabric through his damp hair, shaking off the excess water.

Neither of them spoke at first.

The sound of the water shutting off, the faint drip-drip-drip from the showerhead, filled the quiet instead. Becky took a step toward the bedroom, her bare feet leaving faint, damp prints on the floor, her dark hair clinging in wet strands to the back of her neck. The soft rustle of the towel against her skin was the only noise she made as she moved, rummaging through her dresser for something to wear.

Aaron followed, slower, less certain. He watched her, his mind still half-trapped in the haze of the night before. He hadn't slept—not really. His body had remained still, wrapped around her, but his mind had never settled. Every shift of the house, every whisper of wind against the windows, had kept him tethered to wakefulness, eyes open in the dark.

But Becky had slept.

That was what mattered.

"You okay?" he asked finally, his voice low, cautious.

Becky paused.

Then, slowly, she turned to face him.

For a heartbeat, there was something unreadable in her expression—like she was measuring the weight of her own emotions, trying to decide if they were safe to voice aloud. Then, just as quickly, something changed. Her lips curled into a small smile—delicate, fleeting, but real.

"Yeah," she murmured, her voice quiet but sure. "I think I am."

Aaron held her gaze a moment longer, then nodded. He rolled his shoulders, trying to shake off the lingering tension in his spine, allowing himself the smallest breath of relief.

"Good," he said simply.

And for a moment, it was.

A Morning that Felt Normal, Almost

The scent of coffee filled the kitchen, rich and warm, curling into the air like something tangible. It clung to the space between them, filling the silence with something familiar, something real.

Aaron moved through the kitchen with the ease of habit, but not without effort. Every motion was automatic—the flick of the switch on the coffee pot, the familiar creak of the freezer door as he pulled out the box of waffles, the mechanical motion of popping them into the toaster. But under the surface, there was an undercurrent of exhaustion, a tension he couldn't quite shake.

He hadn't slept.

Not truly.

The night had been a series of half-lucid moments, lying still beside Becky while his mind raced ahead of him, spinning over every possibility. Over the man in the gray hoodie. Over the flickering light. Over what it meant. Over what it could mean.

And yet, somehow, standing in his kitchen, listening to the quiet hum of brewing coffee, the scent of it curling into the air, he almost felt grounded.

Almost.

The toaster clicked.

A moment later, soft footsteps padded across the floor.

Becky.

She stepped into the kitchen, hair damp from the shower, still clinging to the edge of warmth that lingered from it. She leaned against the counter, arms crossed, watching as he moved. Sunlight filtered through the blinds, cutting golden slants across the floor, catching on the soft curve of her face.

She didn't speak at first. Just inhaled the scent of coffee, the warmth of the room settling around her like something fragile, something borrowed.

Then—

"Waffles, huh?" she finally said, a smirk tugging at the corner of her lips. "Just do not burn them this time."

Aaron huffed a quiet chuckle, shaking his head as he poured himself a mug of coffee. "I'll try not to." He shot her a sideways glance, the corner of his mouth quirking up. "No promises, though."

She rolled her eyes but didn't bother hiding the amusement tugging at her expression. "At least the coffee tastes better today."

Aaron took a slow sip, savoring the warmth. Then, with mock seriousness, he let out an exaggerated sigh.

"So, I finally got it right, huh?"

Becky lifted her own mug to her lips, humming in thought as she took a sip. She gave a dramatic pause, then grinned.

"I mean, it's not *great*, but at least it does not taste like burnt dirt."

Aaron placed a hand over his chest in mock offense. "Wow. That's high praise coming from you."

She laughed—a real laugh. Soft, unguarded. It was fleeting, but it was there.

And for just a moment, the weight pressing against both of them lifted.

A Hollow Bite of Breakfast

When the toaster finally popped, Becky peered over his shoulder, inspecting his work.

"I'll be the judge of that," she teased, her voice lighter than it had been in days.

Aaron nudged her playfully with his elbow. "you are just here for the syrup, aren't you?"

She shrugged. "Maybe."

They ate at the small kitchen table, the quiet hum of morning filling the space around them. The warmth of the meal, the soft teasing, the familiar rhythm of it all—it felt fragile, like something that could slip away too easily.

Becky drowned her waffles in syrup, prompting Aaron to raise an eyebrow.

"You want some waffles with that syrup?" he asked, smirking.

Becky grinned, utterly unfazed. "do not judge me. This is the best part."

Aaron shook his head, letting out a chuckle. *This.* This small moment, this piece of normalcy—it felt borrowed. Like something they weren't meant to have, not with everything looming in the background.

And then, just as quickly as it had come, the moment dulled.

Becky hesitated mid-bite.

Her fork hovered over her plate.

Her gaze drifted, her shoulders stiffening as that distant look crept back into her eyes.

Aaron noticed immediately.

He set his coffee mug down, the clink of ceramic against the table cutting into the silence.

"You okay?" he asked, voice softer now. Steady.

Becky forced a small smile, but it was thin, fragile. It didn't reach her eyes.

"Yeah," she said, too quietly.

But her fingers toyed with the edge of her plate, and she was not eating.

Aaron didn't press. Not yet.

Then, finally—

"I'm just... nervous about this psychic," she admitted, exhaling slowly. "What if she tells us something we do not want to hear?"

Aaron leaned back against his chair, watching her carefully. He understood. *God, did he understand.*

"Then we deal with it," he said, voice firm but calm. "Whatever happens, we'll handle it. Together."

Becky inhaled deeply, nodding. But the unease didn't leave her eyes.

And Aaron knew—this weight was not something he could lift for her.

Not entirely.

The Weight of Moving Forward

The rest of breakfast was slow, neither of them saying much. The waffles sat half-eaten on their plates, syrup pooling into the edges, untouched.

Aaron kept an eye on Becky as she pushed the remnants of her meal around with her fork, her thoughts clearly elsewhere.

Finally, she sighed and set her utensil down. "I just do not know if I'm ready to hear it," she admitted.

Aaron nodded, rubbing his palm along the grain of the wooden table. "I get it. But at the same time... we need answers."

She exhaled, leaning back in her chair, staring at the ceiling like it might offer some divine revelation. "What if she tells us there's nothing we can do?"

Aaron frowned. That was not a possibility he wanted to consider. "Then we figure it out ourselves."

Becky huffed a quiet laugh, shaking her head. "You make it sound so easy."

"It's not," he admitted. "But we arenot alone in this. And I'm not letting you face this by yourself."

Becky studied him for a long moment, then reached across the table, fingers brushing over his knuckles. It was a small touch, barely there, but it grounded them both.

"Okay," she whispered. "Let's do this."

Aaron squeezed her hand gently before pulling back, pushing his chair out. "I'll grab the keys."

Becky hesitated before following, her steps slower, more deliberate.

This was it.

Answers.

Or maybe more questions.

Either way, they had no choice but to face them.

Together.

CHAPTER TWELVE

Into the Unknown

A Step Forward

The sound of metal jingling in Aaron's grip felt too final.

The keys were cool against his palm, deceptively light despite the weight they carried. He let them dangle from his fingers, the soft clink of metal filling the silence between them. Such an ordinary thing—keys. A simple tool meant to open doors, to start engines, to take people from one place to another. But right now, they felt heavier than they should, as if they carried something unseen, something neither of them could name.

He hesitated.

His gaze drifted toward the door, its worn brass handle catching a slant of pale morning light. Beyond it lay the world as they knew it—or rather, the world as they had always believed it to be. Rational. Predictable. But after everything that had happened, after the nights spent watching shadows shift in the corners of their vision, after the unspoken things that hovered just outside their understanding, Aaron was not sure that world existed anymore.

Maybe it never had.

He swallowed, shifting the keys in his hand. Then, finally, he turned to Becky.

"Ready?"

The word came out steadier than he felt, but she knew him too well. Knew how to hear the things he didn't say.

Becky stood near the hallway, her arms wrapped loosely around herself, fingers gripping the fabric of her sweater in a way that betrayed the tension coiling just beneath the surface. She didn't answer right away. Instead, she let out a slow breath—deliberate, controlled. The kind of breath meant to steady a racing heart, to push down the doubt clawing at the edges of her resolve.

Her gaze lifted to meet his.

"Let's do this," she murmured.

It was not a declaration. It was not confidence. It was something quieter, something cautious, as if speaking the words too firmly might break whatever fragile resolve she had managed to gather.

Aaron noticed the way her fingers twitched at her sides before she stilled them. The way her shoulders lifted just slightly, as though preparing to brace against something unseen. The way her lips parted ever so slightly before pressing together again, as if tasting the words she hadn't spoken yet.

He could see it all. The fear. The reluctance. The way she was forcing herself forward despite it.

And maybe that was bravery in its own way.

He nodded.

Not because he was ready. Not because he was certain of what lay ahead. But because waiting would not change anything. Because the unknown didn't care whether they hesitated or not. It would be there regardless.

So, together, they stepped into it.

Bound by Shadows

The drive was quiet.

Not the kind of comfortable silence they sometimes shared—the kind laced with unspoken understanding—but thick, dense, filled with the weight of thoughts neither of them voiced.

The low hum of the radio murmured in the background, barely more than static in the space between them. It was just noise, an attempt to fill the silence, to make it feel less suffocating.

It didn't work.

Becky sat rigid in the passenger seat, her fingers twisting the hem of her sleeve, the fabric folding and unfolding beneath her grip. It was something to do, something tangible to ground her against the feeling pressing against her chest.

Aaron's grip on the steering wheel was too tight, his knuckles stark white against the leather. He hadn't said much since they left the house, but his thoughts were loud.

The man in the gray hoodie.

The flickering lights.

The feeling that something was wrong, that they weren't alone.

He exhaled sharply through his nose, forcing his focus back onto the road. They needed answers.

But part of him was not sure if he really wanted to hear them.

When they finally pulled up in front of the shop, Becky's stomach twisted.

It was an old brick building, wedged between a laundromat with buzzing fluorescent lights and an antique store with a CLOSED sign hanging haphazardly in the window. The psychic's shop looked worn, its dark green paint peeling around the window sills, the wood beneath splintering with time.

Above the entrance, a wooden sign swayed slightly in the breeze, rusted chains creaking as they bore its weight. The faded gold lettering was barely legible:

Hannah's Psychic Readings.

In the window, a neon OPEN sign flickered weakly, struggling to hold its glow.

Becky frowned. This is it?

Her skepticism must have been obvious because Aaron cleared his throat, shifting uncomfortably in his seat.

"She helped my aunt when she was going through some... stuff," he explained, but even as he said it, his gaze flickered back to the storefront, like he was second-guessing himself. "If anyone can help us, it's her."

Becky exhaled slowly, eyeing the building with doubt.

"It looks... sketchy," she muttered.

Aaron let out a short, nervous chuckle. "Psychics aren't exactly known for prime real estate."

Becky didn't laugh.

She stared at the entrance, the unease curling tighter in her chest.

Her gut screamed, turning around.

But she unbuckled her seatbelt anyway.

"Fine," she murmured. "Let's get this over with."

The Weight of the Unknown

The moment they stepped inside, the air changed.

It was thick—heavier somehow. The scent of incense clung to the room, curling around them like invisible hands, threading through the air in ribbons of lavender, sage, and something more profound, more decadent.

The dim and purposeful lighting made shadows stretch unnaturally across the space.

Dark purple tapestries embroidered with constellations and moon phases adorned the walls. Strings of fairy lights wove through them, casting a soft, flickering glow. Shelves lined the space, filled with tarot decks, crystals, and small glass jars of dried herbs, each labeled in careful, slanted script.

But Becky's gaze landed on the center of the room.

A single round table sat beneath the warm glow of candles, its surface draped in thick black velvet. A well-worn deck of tarot cards rested beside a glass orb that reflected the candlelight in strange, shifting patterns.

Then—

The beaded curtain at the back rustled.

A woman stepped out.

She was older than Becky expected—her late forties, maybe early fifties—her long silver hair cascading in soft waves around her shoulders. Her sharp blue eyes carried an unsettling clarity, too piercing, too knowing, like she was already peeling them apart layer by layer before they had spoken a single word.

She absently shuffled a deck of cards in her hands, her fingers moving with effortless precision.

Then she smiled—warm, knowing.

"You must be Becky and Aaron."

Becky stiffened, her stomach twisting into knots.

Her voice was sharp, immediate. "How could you possibly—"

Hannah lifted a hand.

"People in your situation do not walk in here without a reason."

Becky exchanged a glance with Aaron. His brows lifted slightly, but he didn't say anything.

Hannah gestured toward the table. "Come," she murmured. "Let's talk."

The velvet fabric beneath Becky's fingertips was impossibly soft, almost too much so. It was the kind of material that absorbed sound. She ran her fingers over it absently, her pulse drumming beneath her skin as Hannah shuffled the tarot deck with practiced ease.

The silence stretched just long enough to become uncomfortable. Then—

"you are carrying something heavy with you." Hannah's voice was smooth, but there was an edge to it—something measured, careful. Her gaze flickered toward Becky. "It clings to you—thick, dark."

Becky's stomach clenched.

Then Hannah's gaze drifted toward Aaron.

She hesitated. Just long enough for Becky's pulse to spike.

"But there's something else..." she murmured, studying him. "you are tethered. Both of you."

Aaron frowned. "Tethered?" His voice was steady, but there was something beneath it. Something taut. "What does that mean?"

Hannah set the deck down. She folded her hands atop the table.

"It means whatever is attached to her has extended its reach to you." She met his gaze, unblinking. "That kind of connection does not happen by accident."

Becky's chest tightened.

Hannah's voice remained calm, deliberate. "A tether is not simply a spiritual attachment—it's an exchange. It happens when two people become... entangled in a way that binds their energy together." She leaned forward slightly, her gaze flicking between them. "Whatever haunts you, Becky was tied only to you—until you and Aaron became... intimate."

The words landed like a gut punch.

Becky's fingers curled into her lap, heat creeping up her neck—not from embarrassment, but from realization.

That night.

It hadn't just been comfort.

It hadn't just been an escape.

It had *changed something*.

Aaron exhaled sharply, rubbing a hand down his face. "So now what?" His voice was calm, but there was something else—frustration, guilt. "Is there a way to break it?"

Hannah tilted her head slightly. "That depends." She turned back to Becky. "The spirit attached to you—does it want something? Or is it simply watching?"

Becky's chest felt like it was caving in.

She had seen him—so many times. Lingering in the distance. In reflections. Outside her window. But he had never spoken and never reached for her.

It was as if he were waiting.

Or warning.

"I do not know," she admitted, voice barely above a whisper.

Hannah's expression darkened slightly. "Then you need to find out." She glanced at Aaron. "Because now, it's not just your burden."

Aaron turned to Becky.

And despite everything—despite the fear, the uncertainty—his presence beside her was steady.

Unwavering.

Becky met his gaze.

And in that moment, she knew.

They were in this together.

CHAPTER THIRTEEN

The Tarot Reading

The Celtic Cross

The air in Hannah's shop was thick with the scent of incense, the candles on the table flickering as if disturbed by something unseen. Becky sat rigid in her chair, her stomach coiled in knots. The velvet-draped table between her and Hannah felt like a barrier between what she thought she knew and what she was about to learn.

Aaron sat beside her, his presence steady, his warmth grounding her against the creeping fear in her chest.

Across the table, Hannah shuffled the deck, the whisper of the cards filling the silence. Her blue eyes gleamed with something unreadable as she studied Becky.

"The Celtic Cross spread is one of the most powerful readings in tarot," Hannah explained, her voice smooth, reverent. "It does not just tell you what is—it tells you what led you here, the challenges you face, and the path that unfolds before you."

Becky swallowed.

"This isn't just a glimpse into the future," Hannah continued. "It's a mirror. A reflection of your mind, choices, fears, and what binds you to the past." She placed the deck in front of Becky. "Cut the cards."

Becky hesitated, then reached forward, her hands trembling slightly as she split the deck. Hannah restacked it, then drew the first card.

The Nine of Swords Upright

The candlelight wavered as Hannah turned over the first card.

A chill crept down Becky's spine before she even saw it.

Nine swords. Hung above a trembling figure curled in bed, her face buried in her hands. The air in the room suddenly felt too thick, pressing in from all sides. Suffocating. Oppressive. Becky's stomach twisted violently as the artwork seemed to reach into her, pulling something raw and jagged from her chest.

Aaron stiffened beside her, his jaw tensing as he studied the card. Even he, who never put much stock in tarot, seemed to feel its weight.

Hannah exhaled slowly. She didn't look surprised.

"Fear," she said simply, tapping a long, ringed finger against the edge of the card. "Paranoia. Anxiety consuming you."

Becky swallowed hard, her throat suddenly dry.

You do not have to tell me that, she wanted to say. I already know.

But Hannah was not done.

She ran her fingers over the card's image, her sharp blue eyes narrowing slightly. "This card represents a mind in chains. You are trapped in your thoughts, Becky. You are feeding your nightmares, reinforcing them with every fearful glance over your shoulder, every sleepless night."

Becky's breath stuttered.

Hannah's eyes lifted to meet hers, piercing and unwavering. "And the spirit that follows you?" she continued. "It is feeding off that."

A shudder tore through Becky.

Of course, it was.

She thought about the flickers of movement in the corner of her eye. The figure standing in the rain, staring at her window. The feeling that she was never alone, even in an empty room.

She pressed her nails into her palm.

"I do not know how to stop it," she admitted, her voice barely more than a whisper.

For the first time, Hannah's expression softened—just slightly.

She turned her gaze back to the card, her fingers lightly trailing over the swords above the grieving woman's head. "These swords? They're not real."

Becky frowned, shifting uncomfortably.

Hannah continued, "They hang above you, but they do not touch you. They are manifestations of the mind. They only have power because you allow them to."

Aaron's voice was quiet but firm. "Are you saying the spirit isn't real?"

Hannah's lips twitched slightly. "Oh, it's real. But the way it haunts her? The way it lingers? That is a direct result of the fear she carries."

Becky sucked in a breath. "you are saying I'm keeping it here?"

Hannah tapped the card again. "I'm saying the more you fear it, the more power it holds over you. And right now? It has all the power."

A sick, twisting sensation coiled in Becky's gut.

Hannah sat back slightly, folding her hands on the table. "This card is telling you one thing: If you want to rid yourself of the spirit, you have to stop letting it control your mind."

Becky shook her head quickly. "That's not—how am I supposed to just stop being afraid of something that haunts me?"

Hannah tilted her head slightly. "You stop by uncovering the truth."

Becky's pulse hammered.

The truth.

She had been running from it.

And the spirit knew it.

Hannah exhaled, tapping her fingers once more against the card. "This reading will show you how to take back control. But you must be ready to face what's buried."

Becky's fingers trembled against the velvet cloth.

She had a sinking feeling that, by the time this reading was over...

She would not be able to run anymore.

Hannah turned over the next card.

The Two of Swords Upright

The second card hit the table like a knife splitting the air between them.

Becky's pulse quickened as she took in the image—a blindfolded woman, sitting in eerie stillness, two swords crossed before her chest, the moon looming high above her, casting an unsettling glow over the water behind her.

Something about the image sent a slow, crawling chill up her spine.

Hannah studied the card in silence for a moment before she spoke, her voice like the slow turning of an unseen key in a locked door.

"You are at a crossroads," she murmured, tapping her index finger against the card. "And this isn't a choice that can be avoided."

Becky's stomach twisted violently.

She didn't like the way that sounded.

Aaron leaned in slightly, his jaw tensing as he studied Hannah's face. "What happens if she does not choose?"

Hannah's gaze didn't waver. "Then the choice will be made for her. And the outcome won't be hers to control."

A cold shiver rippled through Becky's body.

Becky's fingers curled into the velvet tablecloth, gripping it like she needed something solid to hold onto.

"I do not even know what the choice is," she muttered, voice tight.

Hannah arched a single brow, tilting her head slightly. "Not yet."

The psychic's silver hair gleamed faintly in the candlelight as she continued, "This woman sits with two swords crossed in front of her, Becky. She holds them—both—because she knows the decision is hers to make."

Becky swallowed, her throat suddenly dry.

Hannah's voice softened, though the weight of her words only deepened. "This card does not represent a choice that someone else will make for you. It is a burden you must carry yourself. And it will not be an easy one."

Becky's stomach coiled tighter.

Aaron exhaled, his fingers drumming absently against the wooden edge of the table. "So, what—you are saying she has to make some kind of impossible decision?"

Hannah's fingers trailed over the artwork, studying the twin blades in the woman's grasp. "Not impossible. But difficult. And once the decision is made, there is no going back."

The room suddenly felt smaller, suffocating, as if the walls themselves were pressing inward.

Becky licked her lips, shifting uneasily in her chair. "Can you be more specific?"

Hannah met her gaze, her blue eyes gleaming with something unreadable. "No."

Becky tensed.

Hannah gestured toward the card. "I am not here to tell you what choice must be made. I am only here to tell you that when the time comes... you will know. And it will be yours alone to bear."

Becky clenched her jaw, her heartbeat a dull roar in her ears.

She exhaled sharply, shaking her head. "And if I choose wrong?"

Hannah's fingers lightly tapped the crossed swords in the illustration.

"That is the risk of choice, Becky. The swords are equal in weight—one is no lighter than the other. The burden will be the same, no matter which path you take."

Becky felt her stomach drop.

She wanted to argue.

She wanted to say that there had to be another way—a way where she didn't have to make a decision that would change everything.

But deep down, she already knew.

There was not.

Aaron let out a slow breath beside her. "And there's no way to prepare for it?"

Hannah considered that for a moment, then tilted her head. "You prepare by knowing that, when the moment comes, hesitation will not serve you. There is no middle ground. No waiting."

She tapped the blindfolded woman's face in the illustration.

"She cannot see what lies ahead. She can only trust her instincts."

Becky sat in unsettling silence, her eyes glued to the card.

A crossroads. A decision that would demand everything from her.

Her stomach knotted painfully at the thought.

Hannah slowly pulled her hand away from the card, her expression unreadable. "The path is not yet in front of you. But it will be soon."

Becky closed her eyes for a moment, forcing herself to breathe past the unease clawing at her chest.

A decision was coming. A choice that couldn't be avoided.

And whether she liked it or not...

She would have to make it.

The Six of Cups Reversed

The card landed with a soft but decisive sound, yet its weight felt immense.

Becky's gaze flicked to it, her stomach coiling into a tight knot.

Unlike the cards before it, this one looked... gentle. Almost comforting.

Two children stood in a bright courtyard, one offering a cup filled with white flowers to the other. The scene was drenched in warm hues, a moment frozen in time—a reflection of innocence, nostalgia, memories cherished and untouched.

But it was upside down.

Something about that made her feel uneasy.

Hannah sighed, drawing Becky's attention.

Her silver hair caught the candlelight, the flickering glow casting shadows over her sharp features as she studied the reversed image. "This is your warning, Becky."

Becky's fingers tightened against her lap, her knuckles turning pale.

"You are clinging to the past, and it is keeping you trapped."

Becky's breath hitched slightly, and Aaron shifted beside her, his presence warm but tense.

Her voice was quiet, but sharp as broken glass. "What does that mean?"

Hannah exhaled, tapping the card lightly. "This card represents memories—attachments to what once was. When upright, it is a symbol of comfort, of moments you can return to for warmth."

She let the words settle before tilting her head. "But reversed? It is no longer a place of comfort. It is a place of stagnation. A place where you have stayed too long."

Becky's throat tightened painfully.

"You believe holding onto the past is the only way to honor it," Hannah continued, her voice softer now. "But in reality, you are binding yourself to it. And it is binding itself to you."

Becky shook her head almost instantly. "I don't want to forget."

Her words came out raw, instinctive—like a desperate plea.

Hannah didn't waver.

"You do not have to forget," she said simply. "But you must stop letting the past *own* you."

Aaron's voice finally cut through the silence, his tone edged with hesitation and concern. "you are talking about the accident."

Becky flinched.

Hannah nodded. "I'm talking about all of it."

Becky clenched her fists. "I can't just move on from that."

Hannah studied her for a moment, the flickering candlelight reflecting something deep and knowing in her eyes. "Do you believe moving forward dishonors him?"

Becky's breath stalled in her lungs.

Her mind flashed back to that night—to the cold rain blurring her vision, to the way the car had spun out of control, to the moment their eyes met before impact.

To the silence that followed.

Her hands trembled slightly as she exhaled. "I do not know."

But she did.

Hannah nodded as if she expected that answer.

Aaron shifted beside her, his jaw tight with something unspoken. "She feels guilty. That's not something you just... shake off."

Hannah turned her gaze to him. "Guilt is natural. But tell me, Aaron—do you think carrying it like this will help her? Will help him?"

Aaron hesitated. His eyes flicked toward Becky. She refused to look at him.

Hannah sat back slightly, folding her hands on the table. "The spirit lingers not just because of its unfinished business—but because of *yours*."

Becky's pulse thundered in her ears.

"Your grief and your guilt are the chains that hold you together." Hannah's voice softened. "And until you free yourself, neither of you will be able to move forward."

Becky felt like the room had shrunk, like the air had thickened to the point of suffocation.

She looked at the card again, the reversed Six of Cups staring back at her.

She had spent so much time looking back.

Reliving. Replaying. Holding onto the pain as proof that she still cared.

If she let it go, if she stopped carrying it...

Would that mean he was really gone?

Her hands curled into the velvet cloth.

Hannah's voice pulled her back. "This is not about forgetting him. It is about allowing yourself to live."

Becky inhaled shakily.

She wanted to believe that.

But she was not sure she knew how.

Not yet.

THE TOWER.

The Tower Upright

The card landed on the velvet with a finality that sent a shudder through Becky's entire body.

She barely had to look at it to know what it meant.

But she did.

And as soon as her eyes locked onto the chaotic, crumbling scene, a sickening wave of nausea rolled through her stomach.

A tower, struck by lightning, flames devouring its structure, its walls collapsing in ruin. Tiny, helpless figures plummeted from its heights, their outstretched hands reaching for salvation that would never come.

The sky behind it was dark, unnatural, streaked with fire and fury.

Everything about the image reeked of catastrophe.

Becky swallowed hard.

Her pulse pounded against her ribs, her fingers curling against the velvet. The weight in her chest felt suffocating.

She knew what this card was.

She knew what it meant.

And yet, when she whispered the words, they still felt foreign and hollow on her tongue.

"The accident."

When the World Crumbles

Hannah nodded, her silver hair catching in the flickering candlelight.

"Yes," she said simply, her voice steady, unwavering. "This card represents the moment your life was ripped apart."

Becky felt Aaron shift beside her, his muscles tensing ever so slightly.

She could feel him watching her, his concern a tangible weight in the space between them.

Hannah's voice was soft but unrelenting. "But The Tower is more than just destruction, Becky. It is truth, revealed violently."

Becky's breath quickened.

The words felt like a pressure against her chest, tightening, squeezing.

Truth?

What truth?

She hadn't forgotten anything.

She hadn't blocked anything out.

She had lived through that night, over and over and over again, until it was etched into her very bones.

The dog.

The road.

The headlights cutting through the rain.

The figure stepping into the street.

The sickening impact.

The moment she had stepped out of the car, shaking, gasping, the cold rain soaking through her clothes.

The sight of his lifeless body, motionless in the grass.

The blood.

The way his head—

Becky squeezed her eyes shut.

She remembered it all.

So what the hell was Hannah talking about?

Something Still Hidden

Aaron was the first to break the silence.

"You keep saying this was not just an accident," he said, his voice careful but firm. "Why?"

Hannah didn't answer right away.

She studied Becky, her blue eyes sharp, calculating—not in a cruel way, but in a way that suggested she was reading far more than just the cards in front of her.

Finally, she exhaled, her gaze dropping back to The Tower.

"Because The Tower does not simply fall without reason."

Becky stiffened.

"What does that mean?"

Hannah tapped a single ringed finger against the flaming wreckage on the card.

"The past was never as stable as you believed."

Becky's pulse thundered in her ears.

"you are saying—what? That my life before the accident was a lie?"

Hannah shook her head. ***"No. But this event, this destruction—this was a breaking point, not just for you, but for everything connected to it."

Becky's chest tightened painfully.

Aaron's voice was calm, but laced with unease. "You said something was still hidden. What is it?"

Hannah tilted her head, considering him.

Then, finally, she looked back at Becky.

"What are you missing?"

Becky's breath turned shallow.

"Nothing."

She was not missing anything.

She remembered everything.

Didn't she?

The room felt too warm, too close, too suffocating.

She could feel Aaron's eyes burning into her, waiting for her response.

Hannah said nothing.

She only reached for the next card.

And turned it over.

THE EMPRESS.

The Empress Upright

The velvet-draped table was beginning to feel like a battlefield, each card another piece of herself laid bare before them.

When Hannah turned over the next card, Becky braced herself for something dark, something ominous, and something that would coil around her ribs like every other shadow looming over her.

Instead...

She was met with warmth.

The Empress was a striking contrast to the cards before her.

She sat serene and powerful, draped in flowing robes, her head adorned with a crown of twelve stars. Flowers bloomed around her, their petals unfurling in soft, rich hues. Behind her, a lush forest stretched endlessly, bathed in golden sunlight.

Life. Abundance. Creation.

It felt so wrongly placed among the ruins of The Tower, the grief of the past, the fear that wrapped around her like chains.

Becky stared at it. Confused. Cautious.

It didn't feel like her.

Hannah's voice was gentle but firm, her silver hair glinting in the low candlelight.

"You are strong, Becky."

Becky tensed.

Hannah tapped the card with a single ringed finger, never breaking eye contact. "Not in a traditional sense, but in the way you love. In the way you care."

Becky felt Aaron glance at her.

She refused to look at him.

Something about those words made her feel too exposed, too vulnerable in a way that had nothing to do with the spirit that haunted
her.

Aaron's voice was quiet but sure. "She's right, you know."

Becky's jaw tightened. "I do not feel strong."

Hannah's lips curved into something knowing. "That's because
you equate strength with force, with action. But this card?" She traced
the edge of The Empress, her touch almost reverent. "This is the kind
of strength that endures."

She let the words settle before continuing.

"You feel everything deeply, Becky. Your compassion runs through
your veins like fire. You are someone who wants to save, to heal, to
protect. And that is a beautiful thing."

Becky's breath hitched slightly.

But it didn't feel like a strength.

It felt like a curse.

Hannah's expression shifted, her fingers lightly drumming against
the table.

"But compassion is a double-edged sword."

Becky felt her chest tighten.

"There may come a time where you must act against your heart to
survive."

Aaron's gaze darkened, his body tensing beside her. "What does
that mean?"

Hannah's gaze flicked between them.

"It means that strength of the heart is still strength—but it is also
a vulnerability. And when the time comes... you may have to choose
between what you feel and what must be done."

A chill rippled through Becky's body.

She thought of the spirit that lingered in the shadows.

Would she have to destroy him to free herself?

Could she?

The idea turned her stomach, but something in Hannah's expression told her the choice would not be so black and white.

"And if I can't?" Becky's voice was barely above a whisper.

Hannah sighed, folding her hands in front of her. "Then you must be prepared for the consequences."

Becky swallowed hard.

Aaron's hand rested lightly against the table, his fingers grazing hers in a touch so subtle, so unintentional that it almost didn't happen at all.

But it was there.

And it was enough to steady her.

For now.

Hannah exhaled slowly, then reached for the next card.

And turned it over.

The Hanged Man Reversed

The next card landed on the velvet like a silent ultimatum.

Becky's stomach twisted painfully the moment she saw it.

A man, suspended upside down, bound by the ankle. His expression was eerily serene, almost as if he had accepted his fate.

But the card was reversed.

Something about that made Becky's skin prickle with unease.

It felt wrong.

Unnatural.

Like a warning.

Hannah's brows knitted together as she studied the card, her fingers tracing the intricate details of the illustration.

Her voice was low and unwavering.

"The time for hesitation is over."

Becky's throat felt tight.

Hannah tapped the card firmly, the sound sharp against the table. "You are stalling."

Becky stiffened. "I do not—"

"Yes, you do." Hannah's gaze bore into her. "You are refusing to face the truth, Becky. You are waiting, delaying—holding onto the false hope that the answer will come to you without action."

Aaron shifted beside her, his jaw tightening. "Becky's not—"

"She is."

Hannah's words cut through the room like a blade.

The air felt heavy, charged with something neither of them could name.

Becky's pulse pounded in her ears.

Was she stalling?

No.

She was trying to understand, trying to make sense of it all.

But the thought nagged at her.

How long had she been trapped in this cycle?

The fear. The paranoia. The guilt.

The waiting.

Waiting for the spirit to come.

Waiting for answers that never appeared.

Waiting for it all to just... stop.

Hannah leaned forward slightly, her voice lower now, almost a whisper.

"If you do not act, Becky... something else will."

A chill rolled through her body.

Aaron's hand curled into a fist against the table, his knuckles going white. "What does that mean?"

Hannah exhaled slowly, her gaze never leaving Becky.

"It means that the universe will not wait for you. That the spirit will not wait for you. That whatever force is at work here is growing impatient."

Becky's fingers curled tightly in her lap.

"So you are saying I have to do something now?"

Hannah tilted her head. "Soon. Very soon."

Becky's heartbeat was a wild, erratic drum against her ribs.

Her breath felt shallow, uneven.

What the hell was she supposed to do?

Aaron's voice was calm, but there was an edge to it now, a rare flicker of anger beneath the surface. "you are making it sound like she does not have a choice."

Hannah held his gaze, not backing down. "Everyone has a choice. But if she waits too long, she may not like the one that's left for her."

Becky swallowed, her mouth dry as ash.

She wanted to argue.

She wanted to say that she had been trying, that she was not just sitting back and letting this happen.

But the truth clawed at the back of her mind.

She was afraid.

Afraid of the spirit.

Afraid of the truth.

Afraid that no matter what she did, it would not be enough.

Her hands trembled slightly as she forced herself to breathe.

Hannah sat back, watching her carefully, as if waiting for her to catch up to the realization herself.

Becky didn't know if she was ready.

But ready or not...

She would have to act soon.

Because something else was coming.

And if she didn't move first—

It would.

Hannah exhaled, reaching for the deck.

And then, without another word, she turned the next card over.

The Devil Reversed

The card hit the velvet with an almost eerie finality.

Becky's stomach twisted into knots before she even looked at it.

The Devil's gaze bore into her, a monstrous figure looming over two chained souls, their bodies hunched in defeat, their expressions etched with quiet despair.

But unlike the upright version, the card was inverted, the beast's towering presence now flipped, its chains weakened, loosened—offering a chance at escape.

A shudder ran through her.

Hannah's fingers trailed lightly over the card's surface before she tapped it once.

"This is about release."

Becky exhaled, though it did nothing to settle the unease curling in her stomach.

Hannah continued, her voice low and steady.

"The Devil reversed is freedom from the chains that bind you. It is the moment of choice, Becky." Her blue eyes lifted, locking onto Becky's with quiet intensity. "It means you can escape this—but only if you are willing to make the hard choice."

Becky's hands curled into tight fists against her lap.

Aaron's voice was careful, but edged with tension. "What kind of choice?"

Hannah's gaze never wavered. "One that forces Becky to stop running."

Becky swallowed hard, her breath uneven.

"You mean the spirit."

Hannah nodded. "Yes. But it's more than that."

Her finger traced the broken chains on the card, the ones binding the two figures beneath the Devil's feet.

"This is not just about breaking free of a haunting. It is about breaking free from fear itself. From guilt. From the idea that you are powerless in this."**

Becky felt her chest tighten, her heart hammering as the words sank into her like hooks.

"You will have to look the truth in the eye, Becky. And when you do... you will have to make a choice that will not be easy."

Her nails dug into her palms.

Her voice felt weak, small. "What if I do not want to see it?"

Hannah sighed, her lips pressing into a thin, knowing line.

"Then you will remain bound to it forever."

The words slammed into Becky with more force than she anticipated.

Forever.

Was that really an option?

To live like this, trapped in an endless loop of fear and paranoia?

To never be free of the thing that lingered at the edge of her vision, always watching?

To always wonder if this was the moment it would reach out and take her?

Aaron shifted beside her, his fingers flexing slightly.

Becky didn't have to look at him to know he was watching her, waiting to see if she was strong enough to face this.

And for the first time...

She was not sure if she was.

"What If I Can't Do It?"

The words came before she could stop them, raw and unsteady.

Aaron's gaze snapped to her, his brows knitting together.

"Beck."

But Hannah was calm, as if she had been expecting the question.

"Then you will remain shackled."

Becky's breath stilled.

Hannah tapped the card again.

"These chains? They are not physical. They are not forced upon you. They exist only because you allow them to."

Becky felt something heavy and cold settle in her chest.

Aaron's voice was quiet but firm. "She's not doing this to herself."

Hannah turned to him, her sharp eyes reading something beneath his words.

"Aren't she?"

Aaron hesitated, his jaw tensing.

Becky felt the weight of his gaze, but she couldn't meet it.

Because deep down, she knew what Hannah meant.

She had spent so much time running, so much time fearing, so much time refusing to act because she didn't want to face what came next.

And in doing so...

Hadn't she kept herself in these chains?

Becky's hands trembled slightly as she exhaled.

She wanted to argue.

She wanted to say she was not weak, that she was not choosing to be stuck in this hell.

But the words never came.

Instead, she forced herself to nod, even though her insides felt like they were unraveling.

"What's next?"

Hannah held her gaze for a long, lingering moment.

Then, without a word, she reached for the deck...

And turned the next card over.

The Hierophant Upright

The card slid onto the velvet with a quiet certainty, but its meaning felt anything but simple.

Becky's gaze landed on the robed figure, seated between two towering pillars. He held a staff of wisdom, his other hand raised in blessing, while two kneeling figures sat before him, their heads bowed in reverence.

It was a symbol of tradition, of learning, of knowledge passed down.

But something about it made Becky's skin prickle.

Hannah studied the card for a long moment, her blue eyes flickering in the dim candlelight.

Finally, she spoke.

"You will receive guidance soon, Becky."

Becky frowned. "From who?"

Hannah tapped the card gently, her rings catching the faint glow of the candlelight.

"That remains unclear. But the Hierophant represents a teacher, a mentor—a source of wisdom that will present itself to you." She tilted her head slightly. "But whether you recognize it... and whether you accept it... that is another matter entirely."

Aaron's voice was low, contemplative. "So, someone's going to help her?"

Hannah exhaled through her nose, her gaze unwavering. "Perhaps."

Becky felt a chill ripple through her as Hannah's fingers trailed over the ancient-looking figure in the card.

"Or perhaps it will not be a person at all."

Becky's breath hitched slightly. "What else could it be?"

Hannah's voice was calm, measured. "A memory. A realization. A truth long buried."

The words hit Becky like a slow, creeping wave of ice.

Her stomach tightened painfully.

A memory.

She thought of the spirit, of the accident, of the moment she stepped out of the car and saw—

Her throat clenched.

Hannah's piercing gaze settled fully on Becky now.

"You will recognize the truth when it comes."

Becky swallowed, her fingers pressing into the fabric of her jeans.

"And what if I do not want to?"

Hannah's lips pressed into a thin, knowing line. "Then you will remain lost."

Aaron tensed beside her, his fingers twitching slightly against the table.

Becky's chest felt too tight, too constricted.

Guidance was coming.

But what if she didn't want to hear it?

What if the truth was something she couldn't face?

Her heart thundered against her ribs, but she couldn't form the words to push back.

Because a part of her already knew.

She had spent too much time running from answers.

And now?

They were coming for her whether she was ready or not.

Hannah exhaled slowly, fingers resting lightly on the deck.

"One more."

Then, without hesitation...

She flipped the next card.

Two of Cup Reversed

The moment the card hit the velvet, Becky felt a shift in her chest—a tightening, a pulling, a quiet kind of ache that she was not prepared for.

She had been bracing herself for another omen of doom, another warning wrapped in shadows and fear.

But instead...

The image was intimate.

Two figures, facing one another, their cups extended in offering. A bond. A connection. Something delicate, something precious.

But the card was reversed.

And somehow, that made it worse than all the others.

Hannah's gaze flickered between Becky and Aaron.

For the first time, her expression softened.

"You fear loss," she murmured. "You fear being alone. And more than anything... you fear losing something that has only just begun."

Becky's chest tightened painfully.

She didn't move.

She barely even breathed.

But her eyes, completely against her will, flickered toward Aaron.

Just for a second.

And he was already looking at her.

The air between them was thick, electric, filled with the unspoken things that neither of them had dared to acknowledge.

But in that second—

That heartbeat of a moment—

They both knew.

Hannah's voice was gentle but firm, pulling Becky's gaze back to the table.

"The things we run from are often the things we need the most."

Becky's fingers curled tightly into the velvet cloth beneath her palms, her nails pressing against the fabric.

She was not just running from the spirit.

She was running from her own heart.

Aaron shifted beside her, his body tense but his voice steady. "Beck..."

She shook her head before he could say it. Before he could give this feeling a name.

"This isn't about me and Aaron," she said quickly, her voice sharper than she intended. "This is about the haunting. About everything that's happening."

Hannah just watched her, unreadable.

Then, slowly, she reached out, tapping the inverted cups on the card.

"Are you sure?"

Becky felt the weight of those two words sink into her ribs.

She swallowed hard, her mind screaming for an escape.

Aaron's voice was quieter this time. "Becky..."

She couldn't look at him.

She knew if she did—

If she met his eyes again, and saw the same quiet, hesitant longing mirrored in his expression—

She'd break.

So instead, she exhaled sharply, forcing herself to straighten, forcing her voice to steady.

"What does it mean? The reversal?"

Hannah sighed, but there was no frustration in it—only patience.

"It means a connection at risk. Something fragile, something un-resolved." She tilted her head. "Something unspoken that could slip away if left unacknowledged."

Becky's heartbeat hammered in her chest.

She was not stupid.

She knew what Hannah was saying.

She knew what she was pointing to.

And she hated how much it terrified her.

"What if I just... do not deal with it?" Becky's voice was quiet.

Hannah gave her a sad, knowing smile.

"Then fear will steal it from you, piece by piece until there's nothing left to save."

Becky's stomach dropped.

Aaron's hand twitched slightly against the table as if he wanted to reach for her but was not sure if he should.

She wished he would.

She wished he would not.

She wished—

Damn it.

Hannah exhaled, placing both hands over the deck.

"One last card."

Then, without hesitation...

She flipped the final card.

The Sun Upright

The final card landed softly on the velvet, but its impact hit Becky like a breath of air after drowning.

She just stared at it for a moment, unable to process what she was seeing.

It differed from the others—no darkness, chains, or warnings of impending doom.

Just warmth.

A golden sun, bright and unrelenting, dominated the card, its rays stretching outward like open arms. Below it, a child rode forward on a white horse, arms lifted, bathed in light. Behind them, a field of sunflowers stretched endlessly, their petals soaking in the golden glow.

It was a joy.

It was clarity.

It was a future she hadn't dared to imagine.

Hannah smiled faintly, the first true softness Becky had seen in her since the reading began.

"This card is proof that hope is not lost."

Becky's breath came out shaky, her hands trembling slightly as she clenched them in her lap.

Aaron let out a quiet exhale beside her, his shoulders visibly easing for the first time since this reading began. "So... this means she'll be okay?"

Hannah's gaze flickered to him. "If she chooses to be."

Becky's fingers twitched. "What do you mean?"

Hannah tapped the card lightly. "The Sun means clarity, Becky. It means the darkness will not last forever. If you take the right path, warmth, joy, and peace are still waiting for you."

Becky swallowed hard, her throat tight.

She wanted to believe it.

She wanted to believe that there was an end to the nightmare, that this was not just an endless tunnel of fear and pain dragging her down with no escape.

Her fingers lifted slowly, almost hesitantly, grazing the card's edge.

It felt actual, solid beneath her touch.

Could she have this?

Hannah's voice cut through her thoughts before she could answer that for herself.

"Your future is not set in stone."

Becky's head snapped up.

Hannah's expression had shifted again—not cold, not cruel, but measured. Serious.

"This is one possible outcome. But it is not guaranteed."

Aaron's brows furrowed slightly; his voice edged with concern. "So what has to happen for her to get this future?"

Hannah's gaze didn't waver.

"She must confront what needs to be confronted. She must make the choice that terrifies her the most."

The words hung in the air, a shadow against the warmth of the sun's golden glow.

Becky's stomach tightened.

She had barely let the possibility of hope settle before Hannah's voice darkened the moment.

"But be warned."

The room felt too quiet, the candlelight flickering strangely against the deep purple walls.

Aaron sat up straighter, his fingers tapping lightly against the table as if bracing for whatever came next. "Warned about what?"

Hannah's gaze was unreadable. "The sun's light does not come without a price."

Becky felt her entire body go rigid.

"What kind of price?" she whispered.

Hannah exhaled, folding her hands over the table. "The hardest choice still waits for you, Becky."

The words hit her like ice to the spine.

Because deep in her chest, she already knew.

This was not over.

Not yet.

CHAPTER FOURTEEN

The Lesson of the Hierophant

The Hierophant's Truth

Becky's hands trembled slightly as she exhaled, the weight of the reading pressing into her chest like an invisible hand tightening around her ribs. The flickering candlelight cast long, wavering shadows over the table, making the tarot cards appear almost alive. The Hierophant's solemn gaze stared back at her from the spread, his robed figure a stark reminder that guidance had already been given—she just hadn't seen it.

Hannah, still eerily calm, tapped the card with one slender finger. "It already has."

Becky's breath hitched.

Aaron frowned, leaning forward, his forearms braced against the velvet tablecloth. "What does that mean?" His voice was edged with doubt, but underneath it, there was something else—something more vulnerable.

Hannah finally sat back in her chair, her fingers steepling as she studied Becky with an unreadable expression. "This reading was not telling you to *wait* for guidance, Becky. It was telling you to *recognize* it."

A chill rolled down Becky's spine.

"Recognize it?" she echoed, shaking her head. "I do not—"

Then she stopped.

Because Hannah was not just watching her.

She was *waiting* for Becky to understand.

The realization settled over her like a cold weight. She stared down at the Hierophant card again. The robed figure. The knowledge passed down. The role of a teacher.

Her heart pounded.

Slowly, her eyes lifted back to Hannah, the answer forming before she could stop it.

"It's *you*," Becky whispered.

Aaron inhaled sharply, the pieces clicking into place for him as well. "Jesus."

Hannah didn't react, only giving a small, almost imperceptible nod.

Becky felt lightheaded, her mind racing. "You knew this whole time."

"I suspected," Hannah corrected smoothly. "But the cards confirmed it."

Becky swallowed, her throat suddenly dry. "So... what are you supposed to *teach* me?"

Hannah leaned forward slightly, the candlelight dancing in her sharp blue eyes. "I am supposed to tell you how to *end* this."

A chill rushed through Becky's veins.

Aaron's entire body went taut beside her. "End it *how*?"

Instead of answering immediately, Hannah reached into the folds of her robe, pulling out a small, aged leather journal. The spine was cracked, the edges frayed with time. It looked ancient, like it had been passed down through too many hands to count.

She placed it in front of Becky.

"This," she murmured, "is what you need."

Becky hesitated before reaching for it, her fingers brushing over the worn leather. It felt warm under her touch, almost pulsing with energy, as if the book itself was alive.

She carefully opened it.

Inside, the pages were filled with precise, meticulous writing. Rituals, incantations, symbols that she didn't recognize. But more than that—there were *notes*.

Handwritten notes.

Warnings.

Becky's stomach twisted as she skimmed the first line:

"To sever a tether, one must first acknowledge its price."

Her pulse stuttered.

Aaron, peering over her shoulder, frowned. "What the hell is this?"

Hannah exhaled. "A record of those who have encountered this before you."

Becky's fingers tightened on the pages. "Others have... *been through this*?"

Hannah nodded gravely. "Not many. And even fewer survived."

Silence fell between them.

Aaron tensed beside her. "You *could've* led with that."

Hannah's lips twitched, like she found something about that amusing. But there was no humor in her eyes.

Becky flipped through more of the pages. The ink varied, some entries written in elegant cursive, others scrawled in frantic, slanted writing—like the author had been in a rush, like they hadn't *had* time. Some of the rituals were violently crossed out. Others were underlined.

The words '*DO NOT ATTEMPT*' appeared more than once.

Her fingers stilled when she reached the most recent entry.

The handwriting was bold and deliberate.

"The spirit does not want to leave. It will fight. Be prepared to make the choice no one ever wants to make."

Becky's vision blurred slightly.

Aaron's hand settled on her knee, grounding her.

She inhaled sharply. "So what do we do?"

Hannah folded her hands. "You follow what is written. But you do *not* go into it blindly."

Becky's pulse pounded. "What happens if we fail?"

Hannah didn't blink.

"Then it takes you."

The weight of those words settled like lead in Becky's chest. Aaron stiffened beside her, his grip on her knee tightening.

Becky closed her eyes briefly, inhaling sharply. Then she opened them again and looked at Hannah.

"Tell me *everything*."

Hannah nodded.

And the real lesson began.

A Choice No One Should Make

The door chime echoed faintly behind them as they stepped back onto the damp pavement, but to Becky, the sound felt *wrong*—too delicate, too final.

The world outside continued as if nothing had changed. Cars passed by. Pedestrians walked without urgency. Life *continued*.

But Becky felt like she had stepped into another reality.

She hugged her arms around herself as a cold gust of wind cut through the air. The storm had passed, but its aftermath remained—puddles reflecting the gray sky, wet leaves clinging to the pavement, and the thick scent of damp earth lingering around them.

Aaron pressed his key fob, unlocking the car. The beep was sharp, intrusive against the quiet. He glanced at Becky as she stood frozen, staring blankly at the flickering neon sign in the window of Hannah's shop.

The glow pulsed weakly, struggling to hold its light.

Just like *her*.

"Beck?" Aaron's voice was soft, cautious. "You okay?"

She blinked.

Was she *okay*?

No.

But she nodded anyway. "I do not know," she admitted. "That was... a lot."

Aaron exhaled slowly, his breath visible in the cold. "Yeah." He rubbed the back of his neck. "I do not know what I was expecting, but... it was not that."

Becky's fingers dug into her sleeves. "A tether," she murmured. "A choice." She shook her head. "How the hell am I supposed to *choose* something like that?"

Aaron didn't answer right away.

Then, quietly, he said, "We'll figure it out."

Becky turned her head, meeting his gaze.

There was no hesitation in his voice.

No doubt.

Aaron reached out, gently taking her hand, squeezing once. His palm was warm, grounding.

"We'll figure it out," he repeated, softer this time.

Becky inhaled deeply.

She didn't know if she believed him.

But she wanted to.

So she squeezed his hand back.

Wordlessly, they climbed into the car. Aaron started the engine, the heater blasting against the lingering cold.

As they pulled out of the lot, Becky glanced once more at Hannah's shop, watching as the neon sign flickered again.

Then, as the car turned the corner, it vanished from sight.

And the road ahead stretched dark and uncertain.

An Impossible Decision

They drove in silence for a while.

The hum of the engine was the only sound between them, a dull, unchanging noise that filled the space where words should have been. The occasional flicker of neon signs outside cast momentary glows across Becky's face, but she barely noticed. She just stared out the window, eyes distant, fingers tightening and loosening in her lap in an unconscious rhythm.

Her thoughts were a storm, violent and unrelenting.

The reading.

The warnings.

The impossible choice Hannah had laid before them.

It was circling her like a noose, pulling tighter with every second that passed.

Aaron gripped the steering wheel a little too tightly, his knuckles pale against the leather. He wanted to say something—anything—to break the suffocating weight pressing down on both of them. But what could he say?

What words could possibly soften the reality of what they were facing?

The psychic's voice haunted him.

"Whatever is haunting you, it was tied only to you—until you and Aaron became... intimate."

His stomach twisted.

This was not just Becky's burden anymore. It was his, too.

A mile passed. Then another.

Finally, Becky let out a slow breath and shook her head. "I still can't believe she knew."

Aaron flicked a glance toward her. "About us?"

She nodded, rubbing her arms as if trying to shake off a chill that had nothing to do with the cold. "It's not like we walked in there holding hands. And yet... she just *knew*."

Aaron thought back to Hannah's piercing gaze, the way she had dissected them the moment they stepped inside her shop, as if she could read the invisible lines that tethered them together.

"She said it's because we are connected," he murmured.

Becky swallowed, her fingers curling into the fabric of her jeans. "That we... *exchanged* something."

Aaron didn't respond right away. He didn't have to.

The truth sat between them, unspoken but heavy, like a presence all its own.

After a beat, he reached over and took her hand, his thumb brushing softly against her knuckles. "We'll figure it out, Beck."

She turned toward him then, eyes shining with something fragile.

A part of her wanted to believe him.

A part of her *needed* to.

She gave the smallest nod.

The Bluebird Diner

The road stretched before them, empty and dark, the yellow lines blurring as the silence between them grew heavier. It had been this way since they left Hannah's shop, neither of them daring to break the quiet, both lost in the gravity of what had just been revealed.

Aaron's hands gripped the wheel, his knuckles tense against the leather. His mind kept circling back, over and over, to the impossible choice laid at their feet.

A tether.

A spirit seeking revenge.

A price that had to be paid.

Beside him, Becky sat still, her face turned toward the window, but she was not looking at anything. She was not seeing the blurred outlines of streetlights or the occasional passing car. Her hands were clenched in her lap, her fingers gripping the fabric of her jeans like an anchor, and her mind was spinning with thoughts she was not ready to voice.

Aaron finally exhaled, breaking the silence. "Let's grab something to eat," he said, his voice lighter than it had been all day. "We need food. Might help us think straight."

Becky blinked at the suggestion, as if the idea of eating hadn't even occurred to her. She nodded, but it was mechanical, as though she was simply agreeing because she had no energy to argue.

Aaron turned into the small parking lot of The Bluebird Diner, the neon sign above flickering weakly, casting pale red and blue light onto the wet pavement.

The place looked like it had been frozen in time. Checkered tile floors, red vinyl booths, a jukebox in the corner that had probably been broken for years. The smell of coffee and frying grease wrapped around them the moment they stepped inside, a scent that should have been comforting but only seemed to underline the exhaustion sitting heavy in Becky's bones.

A tired-looking waitress greeted them with a small nod, her pen already poised over her notepad.

"Can I get you started with drinks?"

Becky barely glanced at the menu. "I'll take a Coke, and I already know what I want to eat, Grilled cheese and soup."

Aaron hesitated for a half a second before ordering a cheeseburger and fries with a Dr. Pepper, even though the thought of food barely sat right in his stomach.

The waitress scribbled down their order and disappeared, leaving them sitting across from each other in a booth by the window.

Minutes passed.

Drinks came first.

Becky took a sip of her Coke.

Aaron's phone vibrated against the tabletop. He glanced at the screen, muttered something under his breath, and answered.

"Steve, I already told you—check the backlogs first." He drummed his fingers on the table, listening. *"No, that would not cause a full system crash."*

Another pause. Aaron pinched the bridge of his nose.

"Alright. Just keep me updated."

He ended the call, shaking his head as he took a sip of his drink. Becky didn't ask. She figured work never really stopped for him.

The food came.

But Becky barely touched hers.

She stirred her soup absently, her eyes fixed on the swirling liquid, lost in the endless motion of it.

Aaron watched her for a long moment, then finally spoke. "What's on your mind?"

Becky let out a quiet, humorless laugh, shaking her head. "*Everything.*"

Her fingers tightened around the spoon, but she didn't take a bite.

"How are we supposed to make a decision like this?" Her voice wavered slightly, raw and unsteady. "Hannah basically told us we have to choose between dying ourselves or..." She swallowed hard, her voice nearly breaking. "Or *killing someone else.*"

The words sat between them, heavy and undeniable.

Aaron leaned forward, resting his forearms on the table. "we arenot doing anything yet," he said, his voice steady but gentle. "We'll figure it out, Beck. We just... need time."

"*Time for what?*" The words came out sharp, harsher than she intended.

A couple in the next booth turned briefly, but Becky didn't care.

She lowered her voice, her fingers tightening in frustration. "We *do not* have time, Aaron. You heard what she said. It's going to get worse. What if it already is? What if it's too late?"

Aaron didn't hesitate. He reached across the table, covering her hand with his.

"Hey."

Becky stilled.

His grip was firm but comforting, grounding her in a way nothing else had all day. Slowly, she lifted her gaze to meet his.

"we arenot giving up," Aaron said, his voice unwavering. "Not now. Not ever. we aregoing to figure this out. *Together.*"

Becky stared at him, her breath shaky, her chest tight with emotions she was not sure how to untangle.

But for the first time since Hannah's shop, the chaos inside her head softened.

Not gone.

But quiet.

"...Okay," she whispered.

Aaron gave her hand a tiny squeeze before pulling back. "Now eat," he said, nodding toward her untouched soup. "you are no good to me if you are starving."

Becky managed the slightest flicker of a smile.

She picked up her spoon.

It was not much.

But it was something.

Love in the Silence

The drive home was quiet. Not the kind of silence that felt suffocating or strained, but the kind that filled the space between them with something unspoken. Something neither of them was quite ready to name.

Lighter in some ways. Heavier, in others.

The weight of everything still lingered, clinging to them like mist on their skin: the impossible choices, the tether, the unknown that stretched before them, dark and vast. But the fear was not as sharp for the first time all day.

By the time they stepped through Becky's front door, exhaustion had settled deep in her bones, making her movements sluggish and her breath heavier. She barely had the energy to kick off her shoes before she drifted toward the couch, sinking into the cushions like something fragile and weightless.

Aaron locked the door behind them, his fingers lingering on the deadbolt for a second longer than necessary. It was not about the lock. It was about *control*. About doing whatever little thing he could to keep her safe.

His gaze followed Becky, watching how her body folded into itself, small and tired, her head resting against the arm of the couch. He didn't think twice before crossing the room, settling beside her without hesitation.

Neither of them spoke.

Becky leaned into him slightly, and instinct took over. Aaron lifted his arm, wrapping it around her shoulders and pulling her close. She fit against him easily, as she belonged there, her warmth pressing into his side, her steady breath against his chest.

For once, the silence didn't feel unbearable.

For once, it was not filled with ghosts, fear, or the weight of what they didn't know.

It was just... there.

Aaron let out a slow breath, his fingers trailing absent patterns along her arm, tracing soft, invisible shapes against her skin. Becky sighed at the touch, a quiet, content sound, something inside her unclenching for the first time in what felt like forever.

"I'm glad you are here," she murmured, her voice barely more than a breath.

Aaron pressed a soft kiss to the top of her head.

"I'm not going anywhere."

Becky let out a shaky exhale, and then, before she could second-guess herself—before fear or doubt or the weight of everything between them could steal the moment away—she whispered,

"Aaron... I love you."

Aaron froze.

She felt his sudden stillness, his breath hitching, and his fingers paused against her skin.

Her heart pounded so hard it hurt, but she didn't take it back.

She meant it.

She had *always* meant it.

Slowly, Aaron pulled back just enough to look at her. His dark eyes searched hers, something deep and raw swirling in them, something that made her breath catch.

Then, slowly—like he was letting himself believe it—he smiled.

"You have no idea how long I have wanted to hear that."

Becky let out a quiet, nervous laugh. "Maybe as long as I've wanted to say it."

Aaron exhaled, his hands cupping her face, his thumbs brushing against her cheek with something close to reverence.

"Probably as long as I have wanted to tell you the same thing."

Before she could process his words, his lips were on hers.

The kiss was slow. Steady.

Not desperate. Not rushed.

Just *them*.

For a moment, the world outside didn't exist. Not the spirit. Not the tether. Not the impossible choices waiting for them in the dark.

Just Aaron. Just Becky.

The soft press of her hands against his chest, the way his fingers tangled in her hair, the warmth of her breath as she sighed into him as if letting go of something she had been holding onto for far too long.

And then—without a word—she took his hand and led him toward the bedroom.

Tethered by Love

The sheets tangled around them, warmth cocooning their bodies in a way that had nothing to do with temperature. The weight of the day, the fear that had clung so tightly to them, had been momentarily cast aside, lost in whispered words and the slow unraveling of everything they had held back for too long.

Aaron kissed Becky's shoulder, his lips lingering there, his breath steady but deep, as if anchoring himself in her presence. His arms remained wrapped around her, his hold firm but gentle, like he never intended to let go. And he didn't.

Becky nestled closer, her body melting against his, fitting perfectly in the space beside him. She let out a small, contented sigh—barely a sound, more of a release—as if she had finally exhaled all the weight she had been carrying. Aaron felt it happen—the precise moment her body relaxed, the tension wound so tightly inside her finally giving way to exhaustion.

For the first time in what felt like days, she was asleep.

Aaron lay still, watching her for a moment. The soft glow of the moon filtered through the half-open blinds, casting silver streaks across the sheets and illuminating the delicate features of her face. In sleep, she looked peaceful—unburdened. There was no fear, no worry, just Becky.

His fingers absently traced along her arm, barely ghosting over her skin, a silent reassurance that she was here, that she was real, that this was not something that would disappear the moment he closed his eyes.

He had been afraid to sleep before. Fearful of what lurked in the dark corners of his mind. Terrified of what waited for them when they woke.

But not tonight.

Tonight, she had said she loved him.

Tonight, she was safe in his arms.

Tonight, they were together, not just in fleeting moments of shared fear but in something real—something that tethered them far beyond whatever haunted them.

Aaron exhaled slowly and deeply, his hand resting lightly against the small of her back. He felt the warmth of her skin beneath his fingertips.

And for the first time in what felt like forever, he closed his eyes, too.

And as sleep took him, one thought settled deep into his bones—solid, unshakable.

He was never letting her go.

CHAPTER FIFTEEN

A Promise in the Dark

A Warning in the Dark

Becky's breath caught in her throat as she jolted upright in bed, her chest rising and falling in uneven, frantic bursts. It took her a moment to gather her bearings, the heavy fog of sleep clinging to her mind like a suffocating veil. But something was wrong.

The air in the room was thick and oppressive. Cold and suffocating, it pressed against her skin like unseen hands, wrapping around her throat and creeping into her bones. A chill settled deep inside her, unlike anything she had ever felt.

She was not alone.

The weight of an invisible gaze bore down on her, making her skin prickle with something primal and unmistakable.

Slowly—so slowly she could hear the pounding of her heartbeat in her ears—she turned her head toward the shadows stretching across the room. The dim glow of the streetlights outside barely filtered through the blinds, casting jagged slashes of pale light against the ceiling.

Besides her, Aaron was still, his arm draped loosely over her waist, his face calm, untouched by the dread crawling through her. His breathing was steady, his body warm. Blissfully unaware of the terror creeping into Becky's chest.

And then she saw it.

At the foot of her bed.

A severed head.

Her breath hitched in her throat, and ice spread through her veins, freezing her in place.

The man in the gray hoodie.

Lifeless sea-green eyes locked onto hers, wide and unblinking, his mouth slightly ajar, as if caught mid-scream. His face was pale, the raw, jagged stump of his neck glistening in the dim light, dark blood pooling beneath him, soaking into the carpet in thick, inky stains. The metallic tang of copper coated the air—thick, nauseating—filling her nose, making her stomach lurch violently.

She wanted to scream, wanted to run, wanted to wake Aaron.

But she couldn't move.

Then, the head twitched.

A sickening, unnatural movement.

The lips moved, forming silent words she couldn't hear—slow, deliberate motions as if struggling to speak. The eyes never waved. Never blinked.

An then she understood.

It was not just watching her.

It was warning her.

The realization broke her paralysis.

A strangled gasp ripped from her throat, and she lunged toward Aaron, her fingers gripping his arm so tightly that her nails dug into his skin.

"Aaron!" she rasped, her voice raw and barley audible. "Aaron, wake up!"

Aaron groaned, shifting beneath the blankets. His eyes fluttered open, still heavy with sleep. "Beck?" His voice was rough and groggy, but one look at her face sent a jolt of alertness through him.

She pointed, her whole body trembling. "There. At the foot of the bed. His head. He head was just there!"

Aaron shot upright, his gaze snapping toward the spaces she was pointing at.

But nothing was there.

The floor was empty. The blood, the head, the presence—it was all gone. The room was still, except for Becky's ragged breathing.

He turned back to her, his brow furrowed in concern. "Becky..." His voice was cautious. "There's nothing there."

"I saw it," she whispered, shaking her head, her voice breaking. "I know what I saw."

Aaron reached for her, his hands steady as they wrapped around her trembling arms. "Hey, hey, it's okay," he murmured, his voice low and soothing. "It's gone now. Whatever it was, it's not here anymore."

Becky clenched her eyes shut, pressing her lips together, but it did nothing to stop the shudder that ran through her.

"It's never gone," she whispered. "He's never gone."

Aaron pulled her into his chest, his arms encircling her, warm and solid. He held her tightly, his grip grounding her, anchoring her back to the present.

"We'll figure this out," he murmured against her hair, his voice steady, unwavering. "I promise."

She knew she would not sleep again tonight.

Not after that.

Becky stirred, caught in the hazy space between sleep and wakefulness. The warmth of Aaron's body beside her was grounding, but something pulled her toward consciousness—a voice, low and tense.

Aaron.

She barely opened her eyes, just enough to see the dim glow of his phone screen casting faint shadows against the ceiling. He lay beside her, propped up on one elbow, the other hand gripping his phone.

"This really can't wait until morning?" he whispered.

A pause. A sigh.

"Did you try a hard reset?"

His voice was careful, controlled, quiet enough not to wake her—but she was already awake, listening to the strain beneath his words.

Another pause.

"Fine. Just do what you can and call me in the morning."

The call ended with a soft tap of his thumb against the screen. He exhaled slowly, rubbing a hand over his face, the weight of exhaustion settling over him.

Becky shifted, turning toward him, pressing her face against his chest. His arm instinctively wrapped around her, pulling her closer, his heartbeat steady beneath her cheek.

Wrapped in his warmth, she let sleep pull her under once more—uneasy, restless, but safe in the circle of his arms.

Digging Up the Past

The air in Becky's apartment felt different—charged with something unseen.

Aaron stood near the kitchen, one hand gripping the edge of the counter, the other holding his phone to his ear.

"What do you mean it's all gone? That's not possible." His voice was sharp, edged with frustration.

A beat of silence.

"No, I can't come back right now. Just—figure it out."

He ended the call harder than necessary, his fingers lingering on the phone's screen as if debating calling back. Instead, he exhaled, shaking his head, and stuffed the phone into his pocket.

From the couch, Becky watched but said nothing. The morning air felt wrong. Heavy. As if the night had left something behind—a stain, a whisper of something unseen lingering just beneath the surface.

Aaron ran a hand through his hair and sighed. "I'm going to take a shower."

Becky nodded absently, barely acknowledging him as he left the room.

After a moment, she rose from the couch and walked to the kitchen. The silence pressed in around her as she grabbed a mug, filled it with coffee, and took a seat at the table. She wrapped her hands around the cup, but the warmth barely registered. Her mind was still trapped in last night's image—the lifeless stare, the jagged wound, the silent words forming on his lips. It played over and over in her head, a loop she couldn't escape.

Minutes passed.

Aaron returned, his hair damp from the shower, the scent of soap lingering as he set two plates of toast on the table. He slid one in front of her before sitting across from her.

"You need to eat," he said softly.

Becky finally lifted her gaze to meet his. Her eyes were hollow, rimmed with exhaustion. Red. Haunted.

"I can't stop seeing it," she admitted, her voice barely more than a whisper. "Every time I close my eyes, he's there. Watching me."

Aaron reached across the table, his hand finding hers. His grip was firm, steady.

"I'm here," he said. "We'll figure this out. We'll make it stop."

She nodded numbly but barely managed a bite before pushing the plate away.

Then, suddenly—

"We need to find out who he was."

Aaron tilted his head slightly.

Becky swallowed hard. "We need to know why this is happening."

Aaron leaned back, considering, then nodded. "you are right. The more we know, the better our chances of stopping it."

For the next few hours, they sat hunched over Aaron's laptop, sifting through anything that might give them answers—local news articles, police reports, accident records. The storm had left chaos in its wake—power outages, fallen trees, flooding.

But then—

They found it.

An article.

"Homeless man struck and killed during the storm. Identified as Jacob Hayes."

Becky's stomach twisted violently.

Jacob Hayes.

The man she had hit.

The article painted him as a quiet, solitary drifter who had wandered the outskirts of town for years. But the comment section told a different story.

> *"That guy gave me the creeps."*
> *"I swear I saw him talking to himself like he was seeing something no one else could."*
> *"My grandma always said he was cursed. That something was attached to him."*
> *"Once, I saw him standing in the road, staring at nothing. But it was like he knew something was there."*

Becky's breath hitched.

Her hands curled into fists.

"What if he was cursed?" she whispered, barely able to say it out loud. "What if... whatever was attached to him didn't die with him?"

Aaron's jaw tightened. "And now it's attached to you."

Becky swallowed hard, pulse pounding against her skull.

Aaron exhaled sharply, rubbing a hand down his face.

"Then we deal with it," he said, calm but firm. "We stop it."

Becky wanted to believe him.

But deep down, she was not sure that was possible.

And worse—she was not sure it wanted to be stopped.

A Terrible Truth

That night, the house felt wrong.

It was not just the wind rattling the windows or the lingering chill in the air—it was something deeper, something unseen. The air carried an unnatural weight, pressing down on them, thick with an eerie stillness. The silence felt intentional, as if the house was holding its breath.

The dim glow of flickering candlelight stretched long shadows across the walls as Aaron moved around the room, lighting them individually. The small flames cast an illusion of warmth, but they did nothing to chase away the gnawing unease in Becky's chest.

She curled up on the couch, knees pulled tightly to her chest, watching him.

There was something different about how he moved—too quiet or deliberate. As if every step, every motion, was weighed down by something he hadn't yet said.

Something she could feel coming.

Finally, he finished, but instead of returning to her immediately, he stood there momentarily, staring at the flickering flames. His shoulders were rigid, his hands flexing at his sides as he braced himself for something.

Then, slowly, he turned and walked toward her. He sat down beside her, hesitating before speaking.

When he finally did, his voice was quiet. Heavy.

"I'll do it."

Becky frowned, shifting to face him. "Do what?"

Aaron inhaled, his gaze dropping to his hands, which he rubbed together absently. Then, with a slow, measured breath, he looked at her, his dark eyes unreadable.

"I'll give myself to him."

For a second, her mind rejected the words. They felt foreign, impossible.

Then—

Her stomach dropped.

The air vanished from her lungs like an invisible force had stolen it from her chest. A sharp, twisting nausea curled in her gut, making her entire body rigid.

"No."

Her voice came out in a breathless whisper, a denial not just of what he'd said but of the sheer idea of it.

Aaron held her gaze, steady, but resolute. "Becky—"

"No." She shook her head violently, her fingers digging into the couch as she forced the word out again, sharper this time. "Not."

Aaron exhaled, his jaw tightening. "Beck—"

"Don't even say it," she cut him off, her voice breaking as she surged forward, gripping his hands. "You're not doing this. You're not making this choice."

Aaron's silence was like a knife in the dark.

"What other choice do we have?" he finally asked, his voice low, steady. But beneath the even tone, she could hear the quiet resignation—the weight of a man who had already decided.

Becky shook her head, her pulse hammering against her ribs. "We—we can find another way." She was stumbling over her own words now, desperate. "There has to be another way."

Aaron's expression was unreadable. "We tried. And what did we find?" He let out a slow, bitter breath. "Nothing. Nothing. Hannah said this thing wants revenge, and if I can stop it—"

"You can't!" Becky snapped, her voice rising. "You can't just—just throw your life away!"

Aaron swallowed hard, his fists clenching against his knees. "I can stop it."

Becky let out a strangled breath. "No, you can't," she whispered, her voice trembling. "Please, Aaron. Please. do not do this."

Aaron looked at her then, really looked at her—his face strained, his eyes dark with conflict.

"Beck," he said, quieter now, "if it means keeping you safe—"

"I do not want to be safe without you!" The words came out in a sob, her whole body trembling. "I love you, Aaron! I love you too much to lose you! Do you even hear yourself? Do you even understand what you are saying?" Her voice cracked. "you are not making that choice."

Aaron's breath came sharp and uneven, but he didn't speak.

Becky surged forward, grabbing his hands again, squeezing them so tightly that her nails dug into his skin. "You do not get to decide this," she choked out. "You do not get to just—just leave me."

Aaron closed his eyes briefly as if absorbing the weight of her words.

Then he exhaled, his voice rough. "Becky—"

"No!" She shook her head furiously, gripping his hands even tighter as if sheer force could keep him anchored to her. "You do not get just to throw your life away like it means nothing!"

Aaron clenched his jaw, something breaking in his expression. "It's my life—"

"And it's mine too," she whispered, her voice barely more than breath.

Aaron's lips parted slightly, his expression faltering.

"You think you can just leave me?" Her voice wavered, her hands tightening around his. "After everything? You think I'll just be okay?"

Aaron opened his mouth, but Becky didn't let him speak.

"I will never be okay if you do this," she whispered, her voice raw. "Never."

Aaron exhaled sharply, running a hand through his hair. The weight in his face cracked slightly as her words had finally shaken something loose inside him.

Becky reached out, cupping his face with both hands, forcing him to look at her.

Her thumbs brushed against his cheek, her fingers trembling.

"You promise me," she said, her voice unsteady but fierce. "Promise me you won't do this."

Aaron hesitated.

Becky's breath caught, and she swallowed the sob, threatening to break free.

"Promise me, Aaron."

Aaron's gaze flickered—just a flicker, just a breath of hesitation.

Then, finally—

He closed his eyes.

He leaned forward, pressing his forehead to hers. His breath was warm against her skin. His hands slid up to wrap around her wrists, his fingers pressing into her pulse.

"I promise," he murmured, the words fragile, barely more than air.

Becky let out a choked sob and collapsed into him, burying her face in his chest, gripping onto him like he was the only solid thing left in the world.

Aaron held her tightly—so tightly his arms trembled, his fingers digging into her back as if she might disappear if he let go.

For a long time, neither of them spoke.

The candles flickered, their small flames dancing in the darkness.

Their shadows stretched across the walls—

And in the corners of the room, where the light didn't reach—

Something watched.

Waiting.

CHAPTER SIXTEEN

A Name Not Yet Chosen

The morning light seeped through the blinds in fractured slants, cutting across the bed in pale, golden ribbons. Becky blinked slowly, her mind surfacing from a restless, uneasy sleep. For a brief moment, she felt warm—wrapped in the safety of Aaron's arms, the heat of his body radiating against hers, the steady rhythm of his breathing grounding her.

She could have stayed there forever.

But reality was cruel.

The moment her mind fully awakened, it came crashing back. The nightmare. The visions. The unbearable weight of knowing that Jacob Hayes—dead and rotting—still refused to let her go.

Her breath hitched, her muscles tensing involuntarily as the memory of those lifeless, sea-green eyes bore into her once more.

Aaron stirred beside her, shifting slightly. His fingers, lazy with sleep, brushed over her bare shoulder before tightening around her waist, pulling her closer. His lips pressed lightly against her temple.

"Morning," he murmured, his voice low and groggy, still thick with sleep.

Becky exhaled, forcing herself to push the fear aside, if only for this moment. She tilted her head up, meeting his gaze—dark, soft, half-lidded with the kind of peace she knew neither of them truly felt.

"Morning," she echoed, leaning up to kiss him.

His lips were warm and unhurried, a stark contrast to the storm raging inside her. For a moment, they both let themselves believe in the illusion—pretend that the world outside this bed didn't exist. That the horrors waiting for them weren't real.

But they were.

And neither of them could outrun it.

Aaron sighed against her lips before pulling back just enough to rest his forehead against hers. His breath ghosted over her skin, warm, steady. But when he spoke, his voice was heavier, edged with something inevitable.

"We need to talk about it."

Becky swallowed. She had known it was coming.

"I know."

Aaron ran a hand through his sleep-mussed hair, his fingers gripping at the strands like he was trying to clear his head. The expression on his face was not one of fear, but of cold, calculated reality. He was not panicking. He was not doubting.

He was preparing.

"Hannah said we have to find a suitable..." He hesitated, his jaw clenching as he forced the word out. "Victim."

Becky flinched.

The word felt like acid against her skin.

She turned onto her side, pulling the sheets up around her like they could shield her from the weight of what they were saying. "Yeah," she murmured. "Someone who's... flawed. Deeply flawed. Someone carrying their own dark secrets."

The room fell into a thick silence.

Aaron's jaw tightened. He exhaled, scrubbing a hand over his face. "Where the hell do we even start?"

Becky sat up slowly, drawing her knees to her chest. The room felt smaller now, suffocating, like the walls were pressing in on them with each passing second.

She forced herself to speak, even though she hated the words.

"I do not know," she admitted. "But we have to figure it out soon."

Aaron didn't respond right away. He just sat there, his fingers drumming against the mattress, his gaze unfocused.

Then, with a quiet resolve, he reached for his phone on the nightstand. His expression was unreadable, his movements deliberate.

"We start looking."

And just like that, the line they swore they'd never cross began to blur.

The Search for Justification

The kitchen felt colder than usual, though the thermostat hadn't changed. The hum of the refrigerator filled the silence between them, the rhythmic ticking of the clock on the wall, an unbearable metronome to their thoughts.

Becky sat at the table, her laptop screen casting a pale glow against her tired face. The words blurred together after hours of reading, but she forced herself to keep scrolling. Crime blogs, archived news reports, scattered forums discussions—each click dragging her deeper into the dark underbelly of the world they now found themselves in.

Aaron sat across from her, his expression carved from stone. His laptop screen reflected his eyes, unreadable and steady, his fingers moving methodically over the keys. He had always been a problem solver, someone who found solutions through logic reason. But this?

There was no blueprint for this. No right answer.

And yet, he made a list.

Neatly written in his notebook, structured like a twisted grocery list:

Potential Targets:

• Violent criminals (repeat offenders and abusers)
• People with dark past (unsolved crimes and predators
• Someone no one would miss

Becky had stared at the words for too long, her stomach twisting with every one of them.

A "target."

A human life.

She pushed away from the table, pressing the heels of her hands into her eyes. "God, this feels disgusting." she muttered.

Aaron exhaled through his nose, barely looking up. "The alternative is worse."

Becky let out a humorless laugh, shaking her head. "You keep saying that like it's supposed to make this okay."

Aaron finally looked at her then, his dark eyes sharp but not unkind. "It's not supposed to be okay, Beck. None of this okay." He tapped the edge of the notebook with his pen. "But we aren't killing an innocent person. We find someone who deserve it."

As if that made it better.

As if that erased the guilt.

Becky swallowed hard, her gaze dropping to her laptop screen. Another mugshot stared back at her—some man arrested three times for domestic violence, out on bail, charges dropped. The comments beneath the article were filled with outrage, people demanding justice that never came.

Her fingers curled into her palms.

This was the type of person Hannah had meant.

The kind who had already stolen something from someone else.

Her mind warred with itself.

Would this not be justice?

Would this not be right?

She thought of Jacob Hayes, of the way his head had twitched, his lifeless lips moving as if trying to tell her something.

Becky inhaled sharply and slammed the laptop shut.

"I can't do this." She whispered.

Aaron watched her carefully, his gaze unreadable. Then, slowly, he set his pen down.

"You don't have to," he said, voice quieter now. "But we have to do something."

Becky rubbed at her temples, eyes squeezing shut. "How do you even choose?" she asked, barely above a whisper.

Aaron hesitated.

Then, after a long moment, he said, "We start by fining the worse one."

It was the only answer that made sense.

And yet, it was the one that made her stomach churn the most.

A Mind Unraveling

Becky's grip on reality had already been fragile—thin, fraying at the edges—but now, it was unraveling entirely.

Jacob was everywhere.

He was there in the crowds, standing impossibly still while the world churned around him. A sea of bodies passed by, oblivious, their voices blending into an indistinct hum, but Jacob never moved. He lingered at the edge of her vision, his form rigid, unyielding, an aberration in the flow of life.

She saw him in reflections—mirrors, windows, even the goddamn silverware.

She would be washing dishes, hands submerged in soapy water, and catch a glimpse of him in the spoon she was scrubbing. His face—detached from his body, lifeless sea-green eyes staring back at her.

She would pass by a store window, and there he'd be, standing just beyond the glass. Always watching. Always waiting.

She stopped looking in mirrors.

She stopped staring at her reflection for too long because she never knew when he would be there, when his presence would materialize from the shadows, a silent spectator in her unraveling sanity.

At the grocery store, he stood between isles, headless, his decayed body dripping with blood that never touched the floor. The scent of iron clung to the air, suffocating her beneath the artificial brightness of fluorescent lights. Shoppers pushed carts past him, oblivious, their laughter and chatter continuing as if the corpse among them was not rotting in real-time.

She clutched a can of soup in her hand, fingers digging into the label, forcing herself to breathe.

This isn't real.

But the blood was.

It pooled at his feet, thick and black, spreading across the white linoleum, inching toward her. Her pulse thundered. The can slipped from her grip, hitting the ground with a dull, echoing clunk.

"Ma'am? You okay?"

Becky's head snapped up.

A young grocery clerk stood a few feet away, staring at her with mild concern, She blinked, her breath shuddering—

Jacob was gone.

The blood. The body. The horror of it.

Gone.

She swallowed hard, nodding stiffly, " Yeah," she muttered, her voice low and hallow. "I'm fine."

But she wasn't fine.

She was far from fine.

The worst part?

No one else could see him.

Not even Aaron.

No matter how many times she gasped, turned, pointed—no matter how violently her breath hitched or how her body recoiled, Aaron's gaze would land on an empty space.

"There's nothing there, Beck."

He would hold her, smooth a hand down her back, press a steadying kiss against her temple. His touch was warm, grounding, but it was not enough.

Because Jacob was there.

Always there.

And she was starting to wonder if he ever planned on leaving.

Tension and Desperation

Days passed. Their search continued. The tension between them grew.

Aaron, once calm and steady, was becoming agitated and restless.

Becky, once desperate to find a solution, was now beginning to break under the weight of her guilt.

They fought.

Not outright screaming matches, but sharp words, cold stares, long stretches of silence.

"I don't know if I can do this," Becky admitted one night, her voice barely audible.

Aaron clenched his jaw. "Then what do we do?"

She had no answer.

He ran a hand through his hair, exhaling sharply. "This thing isn't going to stop, Becky. Every day we wait, it gets worse. I know it's fucked up, but we don't have a choice."

"We do have a choice," Becky snapped. "We just do not like either option."

Aaron looked at her, his expression unreadable. "So what do you want to do? Die? Because that's the only other outcome."

Becky swallowed hard, her hands trembling. "I do not know."

Aaron leaned forward, his voice softer now. "Beck, I know you are scared. I am too. But if we do not do this, we both die. I can't lose you."

Becky looked away.

Aaron sighed, leaning back in his chair. "I'll find someone," he muttered.

Becky's heart clenched. "Aaron…"

"I'll do it," he said again, more firmly this time.

Becky closed her eyes, fighting the overwhelming nausea building inside her.

She was not sure which was worse—the horror of what they were about to do, or the relief that it would not be her pulling the trigger.

She felt like she was losing a part of herself for the first time.

And Jacob, wherever he was, knew it.

Watching.

Waiting.

Smiling.

CHAPTER SEVENTEEN

A Bargain with Darkness

The dining table was a battlefield.

Scattered sheets of paper lay across its surface—some crumpled in frustration, others covered in frantic, smudged handwriting. Entire sections had been scratched out, names scribbled over so aggressively that the ink bled through the page like open wounds.

It was messy. Violent.

And far too real.

Two laptops sat in the eye of the storm, their dim screens flickering with headlines, mugshots, and criminal records. They cast a sterile, artificial glow over Becky and Aaron's faces—both drawn with exhaustion, both hollowed out by the weight of what they were doing.

They had been at this for hours.

Researching.

Digging.

Hunting.

And now, a list had begun to take shape.

A list of names.

Of people.

Of potential victims.

Becky sat motionless, elbows resting on the table, her fingers tangled in her hair. She stared blankly at the papers in front of her, as if sheer willpower could make them mean something else.

Her coffee sat untouched beside her laptop, long since gone cold.

Across from her, Aaron leaned back in his chair, exhaling heavily as he rubbed his face with both hands. His eyes were bloodshot, red-rimmed from hours of scrolling through police databases, old news reports, and dark corners of the internet they never would have ventured into under normal circumstances.

But this—was not normal.

Nothing about this was normal.

Becky let out a slow breath, her voice a murmur, barely loud enough to be heard.

"I feel like we are playing God."

Aaron glanced up, his expression unreadable. "We do not have a choice."

Becky scoffed, shaking her head. "We always have a choice, Aaron. we are just—" She gestured at the mess of papers between them, her fingers trembling. "we are just trying to find a way to live with the one we are about to make."

Aaron ran a hand through his hair, his jaw tightening.

"Would you rather it be one of us?" His voice was quiet but firm. "Because that's the alternative, Becky."

She had no answer.

They both knew what Hannah had told them—a life for a life.

The weight of that truth pressed down on her, made her chest tight, and made her breathing feel harder. It was not just about choosing who deserved to die.

It was about whether they could live with killing.

Aaron inhaled deeply, grounding himself. Then, with forced composure, he picked up the first sheet of paper from the pile.

"Alright," he said, his voice tense but steady. "Let's go through them. One by one."

Becky swallowed and nodded.

She didn't trust herself to speak.

The List

Aaron cleared his throat, reading the first name aloud.

1. Charles Renshaw — Landlord with multiple allegations of tenant
   abuse and exploitation.
· Multiple complaints of illegal evictions, intimidation, and even
   physical violence against tenants who couldn't pay rent on time.
· Several of his properties had been condemned, yet he continued
   collecting payments from desperate renters.
· Had been investigated multiple times but never charged.

Becky chewed on her lip, hesitant. "I mean... he's awful. But is that
enough?"

Aaron exhaled, setting the paper down. "Enough for who? For us
to feel okay about it? For Jacob to accept it?"

Becky shook her head, pressing her palms to her temples. "I do
not know... it feels wrong."

Aaron silently drew a thick line through Charles's name.

2. Terry Whitman — Repeat domestic abuser, arrested multiple
   times but always managed to avoid real consequences.
· Restraining orders from two ex-wives, both of whom had suffered
   serious injuries at his hands.
· Recently accused of assaulting a new girlfriend, but she refused to
   press charges.
Long history of violence, yet never seemed to face real justice.

Aaron tapped the name with his pen. His voice was colder now. "This guy deserves to die."

Becky hesitated. "He does. But... what if he stops? What if he changes?"

Aaron's stare was incredulous. "Do you really think men like him change?"

She bit her lip, looking away.

Aaron sighed, but after a long moment, he crossed Terry's name off the list.

3. David Larson — Former cop involved in multiple brutality cases.

· Several allegations of excessive force, but no convictions.

· Got away with shooting an unarmed teenager—the case was quietly buried.

· Still carried himself like he was untouchable.

Becky clenched her fists.

"Him. He's—" She stopped herself.

Aaron looked up. "What?"

She swallowed, her voice thick. "I hate him. I hate people like him. But do we kill him just because we hate him?"

Aaron leaned back, his expression unreadable.

Then, wordlessly, he crossed Jacob Larson off the list.

4. Henry Turner - Suspected in connection with the disappearances and murders of several victims.

· The victims were said to be homeless or hitchhikers in need of a ride.

· He is suspected of seeking out his victims on the side of the road, portraying the role of a Good Samaritan.

No last known location. He has likely fled the state or even the country.

Becky leaned forward, skimming the notes again, her fingers drumming lightly against the table. Her stomach twisted as she read over the
details, the words painting a picture of a predator who operated under
the guise of kindness.

"He preys on people who already have nothing," she murmured,
her voice tight. "People who trust him because they do not have a
choice."

Aaron exhaled sharply, shaking his head. "It's perfect, in a sick way.
No one's looking for them. No one's waiting at home wondering why
they didn't show up for dinner." His fingers curled into a fist against
the table. "Bastard knows exactly who to target."

Becky swallowed hard, tracing the name with her fingertip. "It fits."

Aaron nodded, but his expression darkened. "Yeah. The problem
is, we do not even know if he's still in the country, let alone where to
find him."

Becky leaned back in her chair, rubbing her temples. "So what do
we do? ... cross him off the list?" The words tasted bitter.

Aaron frowned, thoughtful. "He's the closest thing to a perfect
candidate so far. But if we can't find him, it does not matter."

Becky let out a slow breath, staring at Henry Turner's name as if she
could wait for the answer to appear. "It's frustrating. Knowing he's
out there. Knowing he's probably still doing this."

Aaron's jaw tightened. "Yeah. But we can't go hunting ghosts. We
need someone we can get to." He hesitated, then sighed. "Cross him
off."

Becky hesitated momentarily before picking up the pen and drawing a thick, deliberate line through the name. It felt wrong. Like letting a monster slip back into the darkness.

She set the pen down and stared at the crossed-out name, a knot forming in her chest.

"I hope he runs into the wrong person one day," she muttered, voice low.

Aaron glanced at her, then at the paper. His voice was quieter, heavier. "Yeah," he said. "I hope he does, too."

5. Brian Calloway – Local ex-convict with a history of extreme violence.

· Served ten years for aggravated assault and attempted murder.

· Suspected in multiple unsolved disappearances.

· Recently arrested for nearly beating a man to death outside a bar.

Known for being sadistic, cruel, and completely remorseless.

They both stared at the name in silence.

Aaron set down his pen. His voice was steady, almost too steady. "I think this is the one."

Becky felt sick.

Her fingers curled around the edges of the paper, the weight of the decision pressing into her chest like a stone. She tried to swallow, but her throat was tight. "Aaron…" Her voice barely carried across the space between them. "Are we really doing this?"

Aaron exhaled, leaning back in his chair. He ran a hand through his hair, his fingers dragging through the strands before settling at the back of his neck. He looked at her, his eyes dark with something unreadable. "Beck, we do not have a choice. You saw the list. The others—" he hesitated, then shook his head. "They weren't right. But this guy? He's a monster."

Becky's stomach twisted. She glanced down at the name again, at the history that made her skin crawl. "I know that" she murmured. "But knowing it and..." she trailed off, pressing her lips together. "This is different. we arepicking someone to die."

Aaron's jaw tightened, but his voice was quiet when he spoke. "You think he would not have been picked eventually?"

Becky looked up, startled by the certainty in his tone.

Aaron leaned forward, resting his forearms on the table, his eyes locked on hers. "Come on, Beck. Guys like him. They do not stop. They do not get better. They do not wake up one day and decide they do not want to hurt people anymore." His fingers tapped against the tabletop, slow and deliberate. "He spent ten years in prison, got out, and the first thing he did was nearly kill someone. And that's just what we know about."

Becky swallowed hard, glancing back at the notes. The list of suspicions. The things that had never been proven, the people who had gone missing, their stories swallowed up by the cracks in the system.

Aaron's voice softened, but there was something heavy behind it. "How many more people does he get to hurt before someone stops him?"

Becky exhaled slowly, her hands clenched into fists in her lap. "It shouldn't be us," she whispered.

Aaron's eyes didn't waver. "But it is us."

The silence stretched between them, thick with unspoken things. Becky could feel her pulse in her throat and hear the faint ringing in her ears—the weight of it all, the finality, the choice that would change everything.

Finally, Aaron sat back, rubbing his jaw. "I'm not saying it's easy. Hell, I feel like I will throw up just thinking about it." He let out a breath, shaking his head. "But if we do not pick him, then what? Do we just wait? Hope that something else comes along?" He met her gaze again, his expression softer now, but no less firm. "We do not have that kind of time, Beck."

She bit her lips so hard it nearly hurt. She knew he was right. She hated that he was right.

Becky closed her eyes for a brief second, inhaling deeply. Then, slowly, she reached for the pen. Her hand trembled slightly as she tapped it against the paper.

"We do not know for sure," she said, almost begging for a reason to hesitate. "What if—"

Aaron cut her off, voice low but unyielding. "We do."

She looked up at him.

His expression was resolute. "We know."

Becky's grip on the pen tightened.

A deep breath.

Then, in one swift, final motion—

She drew a circle around Brian Calloway's name.

The Watcher

Becky and Aaron followed Brian Calloway's movements for the next several days, their lives narrowing to the slow, methodical act of observation. Their world became one of watching, waiting, and dissecting every step he took and every interaction he had.

From across the street, Becky sat in the passenger seat of Aaron's car, gripping a disposable coffee cup that had long since gone cold. She barely noticed the bitter taste anymore. Her focus was on the man they had chosen.

Brian's apartment was a rundown complex with peeling paint and a cracked sidewalk, the kind of place where no one asked questions. They watched as he came and went, his routine surprisingly predictable for someone so volatile. Morning meant work—a local auto shop on the edge of town. Evening meant beer—too much of it. And in between, there was nothing but aggression simmering just beneath the surface.

Aaron handled most of the close surveillance. He would sit in his car outside the auto shop, watching through the windshield as Brian yelled at his coworkers, shoving tools and slamming doors. He would follow him to the bars at night, sitting in the corner of whatever dimly lit dive Brian chose that evening. Always the same pattern—too much to drink, too quick to anger, too eager to hurt someone.

Becky kept her distance. She was not built for the close-up work the way Aaron was. She could barely stomach watching from afar but forced herself to stay. To see.

Because seeing means knowing.

And knowing meant she could not deny that they were right.

A Monster in the Making

Aaron's reports were always the same.

"He does not even try to hide it," he muttered one night, slumping into the driver's seat after leaving the bar. The smell of beer and sweat clung to his clothes, but he hadn't been drinking—just breathing in the filth of the place. His hands gripped the steering wheel, knuckles white. "It's not just that he's violent. It's like he enjoys it."

Becky glanced at him, her stomach twisting. "Did he hurt anyone tonight?"

Aaron exhaled through his nose, shaking his head. "Not physically. But he shoved some waitress so hard she nearly dropped her tray. Screamed in her face because he thought she was taking too long." His fingers tapped anxiously against the wheel. "She just stood there, Beck. Like she was used to it."

Becky looked down at her lap, her fingers curling into fists. "How many times has he done this?"

Aaron didn't answer right away. He just stared out at the windshield, watching the rain bead and slide down the glass. When he finally spoke, his voice was low, distant. "Enough that no one even reacts anymore."

Becky swallowed hard.

The more they watched, the more it became impossible to separate the man from the monster.

Brian Calloway was not a question of *if* he would hurt someone again. It was *when*.

Jacob Waits

But they weren't the only ones watching.

Becky saw him constantly now. Jacob Hayes.

At first, it was just glimpses—the flicker of a shadow in the corner of her vision, a shape standing just beyond the streetlights. But as the days passed, he was there more—longer. Clearer.

She didn't know how to explain it to Aaron—how every time she blinked, Jacob was standing in the periphery, headless, motionless, waiting.

She didn't want to explain it.

Because it made it real.

And then, one night, it changed.

They were outside another bar, parked across the street. Brian was in his usual spot at the counter, nursing a drink while his eyes darted around the room, looking for trouble. Aaron was tense beside her, his fingers tapping against the dashboard, his jaw clenched as he watched.

Becky was not looking at Brian.

She was looking at Jacob.

Standing just inside the bar.

Next to Brian.

Her breath caught in her throat.

Not behind him. Not in the distance. Not flickering in and out of view like a trick of the light.

Right next to him.

The ghost's posture was unchanged—rigid, unnatural, his headless form looming over Brian like an executioner.

A rush of nausea swept through her.

This was it.

Jacob was waiting.

Becky grabbed Aaron's wrist, her fingers digging in so hard she barely noticed his startled flinch. Her voice came out hoarse. "Aaron. Look."

Aaron turned, following her gaze.

And for the first time—the very first time—he stiffened.

His breathing slowed. His fingers twitched.

Because he saw it, too.

Jacob was not just watching anymore.

He was ready.

CHAPTER EIGHTEEN

Breaking Point

Becky's house felt too small.

The walls, the ceiling, the very air—it all pressed in on her, suffocating, squeezing like an unseen force trying to crush her from the inside out.

Her pacing had turned frantic, her arms wrapped tightly around herself as though she could physically hold herself together. But it was not working. Her skin was crawling, her breath coming too fast, too shallow.

This was wrong.

All of it.

Her voice trembled when she finally spoke. "I do not know if I can do this."

The words felt foreign leaving her mouth. Like they belonged to someone else, like some other version of her—a better version—was trying to claw its way to the surface, begging her to stop this before it was too late.

But it was already too late.

She shook her head violently, as if she could physically reject the reality of what they were planning. "we aretalking about murder, Aaron."

Aaron sat on the couch, elbows resting on his knees, fingers laced together like he was trying to keep them from shaking. His face was unreadable, his voice firm but quiet. We are talking about survival."

Becky turned sharply, eyes burning. "You say that like we arebetter than him. Like we arenot just making an excuse to do something horrible."

Aaron met her gaze without flinching. "He's a monster, Becky."

Becky let out a harsh, bitter laugh. The sound felt wrong in her throat. "So are we."

Aaron exhaled, leaning back, his jaw tight. "Would it be easier if it was me?"

The question hit her like a slap.

Becky's brow furrowed. "What?"

Aaron's voice was eerily calm. "If I was the one who had to do it. If you didn't have to be involved at all."

A sick wave of nausea rolled through her. "Aaron, stop—"

"I'm serious." His eyes were dark, almost vacant, like the weight of this was finally dragging him into the abyss. "You do not have to do anything. Just tell me you are okay with it, and I'll take care of the rest."

Becky felt her knees buckle. She sank onto the couch beside him, her hands pressing into her face, trying to ground herself, trying to stop the shaking, trying to breathe.

"I do not want this." Her voice was barely a whisper. "I never wanted this."

She felt Aaron's hand on her knee. A steady weight. A silent promise.

"I know."

Silence settled between them.

Not peace.

Not understanding.

Just silence.

A shared, inescapable truth stretched out between them, thick and suffocating. They weren't the same people they had been weeks ago. They weren't even the same people they had been yesterday.

They weren't Becky and Aaron anymore.

They were something else now.

Something unrecognizable.

Something ruined.

And somewhere out there, completely unaware of the fate that had already been decided for him—

Brian Calloway was a dead man walking.

CHAPTER NINETEEN

Setting the Trap

The plan had to be perfect.

There was no room for hesitation, no margin for error. If they were going to do this, if they were truly crossing this line, then every detail had to be precise.

It had to be quick.

It had to be clean.

And, most of all, it had to work.

Becky and Aaron spent the next two days suffocating under the weight of their preparations. The air between them was thick, heavy, filled with words they couldn't say, thoughts they couldn't voice. Every moment was consumed by details, by logistics, by the knowledge that there was no coming back from this.

The instructions Hannah had given them were explicit, brutal. The ritual required more than just death—it demanded suffering. The victim had to die in terror, in agony, their pain serving as an offering to the entity waiting in the shadows.

Becky had nearly vomited when she read that part.

It was not enough to just kill him.

He had to *break*.

It was grotesque.

It was inhuman.

It was necessary.

That was the part Aaron kept repeating. *It's necessary, Becky. It's the only way.*

But necessary didn't make it right.

She sat at the dining table, staring at the crumpled pages of Hannah's notes, her fingers tracing over the ink that had smudged under the sweat of their nervous hands. Every time she blinked, she saw Brian Calloway's name at the top of their list, the final name, the one they had settled on after long, sleepless nights of deliberation.

She tried to convince herself that he deserved it. That this was not the same as murder. That Brian was a violent man, a sadist, a predator who had left a trail of broken bodies in his wake.

If they did this, they would not just be saving themselves.

They would be stopping him from hurting someone else.

It didn't make her feel any better.

Aaron was the one who made contact.

A burner phone, an untraceable number, a carefully fabricated lie. He had posed as an acquaintance of one of Brian's old associates, dangling the promise of a lucrative, under-the-table job. It hadn't taken much convincing—Brian was greedy, reckless, and too arrogant to suspect a trap. He had taken the bait with ease.

The meeting was set for midnight.

A long-abandoned warehouse on the outskirts of town, tucked away where no one would hear the screams.

It was perfect.

Silent.

Isolated.

Untouched by prying eyes.

It was the perfect place to kill a man.

The Night Ritual

The wind howled through the skeletal remains of the abandoned warehouse, rattling the broken windows and whistling through the rusted metal beams overhead. Becky shivered despite her thick jacket, her fingers twitching as she zipped it up to her chin. The air smelled of wet pavement, motor oil, and something darker—something rotten, decayed.

Aaron stood beside the car, his stance rigid, his fingers wrapped so tightly around the burner phone in his palm that his knuckles had turned white. He checked his watch, then exhaled sharply, breath curling like smoke in the cold.

"He'll be here soon," he muttered, voice flat, emotionless.

Becky swallowed hard, her throat dry as dust. She nodded, but the motion felt mechanical, detached from the rising panic clawing at her insides.

Behind them, the warehouse loomed—an open wound in the night, its rusted frame stretching toward the sky like the ribs of a long-dead beast. The darkness inside was absolute, impenetrable. It swallowed everything. Even sound seemed thinner within its walls, as if the air itself refused to carry noise.

Inside, the ritual site had already been prepared.

A crude circle of salt and blood stained the cold concrete floor, jagged symbols carved deep into the walls with the blade of a hunting knife. The markings seemed to pulse under the flickering glow of candlelight, shifting whenever Becky looked at them directly. The air inside the circle felt wrong—thick, charged, like a breath held too long in the lungs.

In the center sat a large, rusted metal drum, half-filled with a thick, foul-smelling mixture of animal blood and the other ingredients Hannah had listed in her instructions—graveyard dirt, bone ash, a scrap of something that once belonged to Jacob Hayes.

The stench made Becky's stomach churn.

She pressed a hand to her mouth, forcing herself to breathe through her nose.

Aaron noticed.

His fingers brushed against her arm—just a small touch, light but grounding. When she looked at him, his expression was unreadable, but his eyes were sharp, steady.

"we arealmost there," he murmured. "Just hold on."

Becky gave a stiff nod, but she was not sure she believed him.

She was not sure she believed any of this.

And then—

Footsteps.

Slow. Measured. Confident.

Becky turned, her pulse hammering.

A shadow emerged from the darkness beyond the warehouse doors, broad shoulders cutting a silhouette against the dim glow of the streetlights outside. He moved with an easy swagger, unaware—so blissfully unaware—of what was waiting for him inside.

Brian Calloway had arrived.

The Offering

Brian Calloway moved like a man who had never had to fear anything. His broad frame cut a confident silhouette against the dim glow of the distant streetlights, his boots crunching lazily over gravel as he approached. His posture was relaxed, his head held high.

Completely unsuspecting.

Aaron tightened his grip on the tire iron resting at his side, forcing himself to keep his breathing even. He couldn't afford to give away anything. Not yet.

Brian's sharp eyes flicked between them as he came to a stop a few feet away. His gaze lingered on Becky, assessing. A slow smirk tugged at the corner of his mouth.

"You the guy?" he asked, voice low and gruff. Then, with a nod toward Becky, "Who's she?"

Aaron forced a casual chuckle, keeping his tone light. "Partner in the job. Hope that's not a problem."

Brian grunted, unconcerned. "Long as I get paid, I do not give a fuck."

Becky swallowed hard, fighting the nausea rising in her throat. She could feel the weight of this moment pressing down on her, suffocating her. Her skin felt too tight, her heartbeat too loud.

Aaron motioned toward the warehouse, his fingers flexing. "Let's go inside. Safer in there."

For the first time, Brian hesitated. Just for a second. Some distant instinct flared in the back of his mind, an old, primal warning. But then he shrugged and started walking, dismissing the flicker of doubt before it could fully form.

They stepped into the darkness together.

A Deal Sealed in Blood

The air changed the second they crossed the threshold.

The warehouse swallowed them whole, the outside world disappearing behind them. The heavy metal door groaned shut, trapping them in flickering candlelight and silence so thick it hummed.

The temperature plummeted.

The shadows stretched unnaturally along the walls, flickering with a life of their own. The salt circle, the symbols carved into the concrete—it all pulsed with something unseen, something hungry.

Jacob was here.

Waiting.

Brian sniffed, his nose wrinkling in disgust. "The fuck is that smell?"

Becky felt like she was drowning in fear, her pulse a frantic drumbeat against her ribs.

Aaron moved.

Fast.

Before Brian could react, Aaron swung the tire iron hard.

The impact landed squarely against Brian's knee with a sickening crack.

A sound that was more wet than it should have been.

Brian let out a roar of pain as his leg buckled. He collapsed onto the ground, his hands instinctively grasping at his knee, his face contorted in shock.

"The FUCK—"

The second blow caught him across the face, the metal colliding with flesh and bone. Blood sprayed from his nose, a splatter of red against the cold concrete. His body crumpled onto his back, his breath coming in ragged, stunned gasps.

Becky stood frozen.

She could hear herself breathing—too fast, too shallow. Her vision blurred at the edges. This is happening. Oh, God, this is happening.

Aaron dropped the tire iron with a dull clang. He didn't hesitate as he reached for the hunting knife strapped to his belt, the steel catching the dim light. His voice was urgent, sharp.

"Help me hold him down."

Becky didn't move.

She couldn't move.

"Becky!" Aaron snapped, the desperation in his voice cutting through the fog in her mind.

Somehow, she forced her body to respond. Her limbs felt weak, shaky, but she moved. Kneeling beside them, she pressed down on Brian's shoulder as he thrashed weakly beneath her.

His eyes—wild, unfocused, filled with something that was not fear yet—locked onto hers. Blood streamed down his face, pooling at the corners of his mouth as he spat at her.

"You fucking psycho." His voice was slurred, thick with pain. "You think you can just—"

Aaron drove the knife into his side.

Brian screamed.

A sound raw and ragged, something animalistic, something that ripped through the stale air and sent chills crawling up Becky's spine. His body arched violently against the pain, his limbs jerking in protest.

The blood came fast.

Hot, dark, seeping over Aaron's hands, pooling onto the floor, spreading toward the salt circle like it had been waiting for it.

The air around them shifted.

The candle flames shivered, stretching unnaturally high before bending in toward the circle. The shadows rippled along the walls, expanding, pulsing.

Something moved in the dark.

A whisper—not a sound, but a feeling—slid down Becky's spine. Cold, wet, slick with malice.

Jacob was coming.

The Ritual Begins

Hannah had given them the words—the incantation, the key to unlocking whatever nightmare they were about to unleash. Becky and Aaron had memorized them, practiced them, and whispered them in the dark when sleep refused to come. But now, standing at the edge of the unknown, those words felt like lead in Becky's throat.

She couldn't breathe.

Her hands were slick with blood—Brian's blood—hot and pooling over her fingers as she fumbled for the ceremonial bowl. The rusted metal was ice cold against her skin, the thick animal blood inside sloshing over the edges as she tried to steady herself.

Brian's muffled screams clawed at the air, raw and frantic. Aaron pressed a firm hand over his mouth, holding him down with a strength Becky didn't know he had.

"Becky," Aaron's voice cut through the chaos, urgent and unwavering. His eyes locked onto hers, dark and desperate. "Say it."

Her stomach twisted.

She could feel it.

Something in the air had shifted. The shadows in the warehouse stretched unnaturally, curling inward, pulsing like they were breathing. The temperature had plummeted, cold biting at her exposed skin like unseen fingers wrapping around her throat.

She had to do this.

Swallowing against the bile rising in her throat, Becky forced the words out, her voice barely a whisper at first. The syllables twisted on her tongue, thick and guttural, ancient syllables bleeding into one another like they were never meant to be spoken by human lips.

"We call upon the forsaken, the bound and forgotten.
Through blood and suffering, we open the path.
By death's embrace, we sever the chains of the restless.
Come forth, oh vengeful one.
Take what is owed.
Claim what is yours.
Through this sacrifice, let the curse be undone."

The air shuddered around them.

The floor trembled beneath their feet.

The warehouse groaned as if it were alive.

The distant sound of thunder rolled through the walls, except it was not thunder.

It was laughter.

A deep, wet, inhuman laughter that seeped from the darkness, filling every corner of the room. It was the sound of something ancient, something waiting, something hungry.

Becky's breath hitched.

Jacob had heard her.

And he was coming.

A chill ran down her spine as the shadows thickened, coiling like living things. The candles flickered wildly, their flames stretching unnaturally high before snuffing out all at once.

Then—he was there.

More vivid than ever before.

More real.

Jacob's headless form twitched in the darkness, his movements jerky and unnatural, like a marionette controlled by unseen hands. Blood dripped from the ragged stump of his neck, but it never hit the floor. It just hung there, suspended in the air as if gravity had no claim over it.

The air smelled of rot.

Of damp earth and something wrong.

A low, vibrating hum filled the room—like a growl, like a voice just on the edge of hearing.

Brian's terrified gaze darted around, frantic, searching. He could see him now.

"No," Brian rasped, his breath coming in sharp, panicked bursts. His chest heaved. His muscles spasmed beneath Aaron's grip. "What the fuck—"

Aaron didn't give him a chance to finish.

The knife plunged into Brian's chest.

A wet, sickening sound filled the room as the blade sank deep, sliding through flesh and muscle like butter. Brian's body jerked violently, his back arching off the floor as a strangled gurgle escaped his throat.

Then—Jacob moved.

Fast.

Faster than he ever had before.

He lunged forward, his twitching, decayed body colliding with Brian's like a shadow slipping into flesh.

Becky screamed.

Brian's ragged screams reverberated through the warehouse, wild and unhinged. His entire body spasmed in Aaron's grip, his tendons straining as if he were trying to rip himself free from existence itself. Sweat mixed with the blood streaking down his face, his eyes darting wildly, searching for an escape that didn't exist.

Jacob loomed over him—a shadow given shape, given hunger. The warehouse seemed to bend around him, the walls pressing inward, trapping them in a space that no longer felt tethered to the real world. The air thickened, heavy and damp, clinging to Becky's skin like oil.

And then Jacob twitched.

His movements were jerky, unnatural, like a corpse reanimated by strings pulled from the dark. His hands—long, skeletal, fingers too sharp and too many—curled at his sides, flexing like a predator preparing to strike. The raw stump where his head should have been moved, the gaping wound pulsing like something alive.

Brian whimpered.

Jacob leaned closer, his entire form vibrating as if his body was barely holding together. A guttural hum resonated from the stump, wet and ragged, shifting the air like a heartbeat outside a body. Becky's stomach turned.

Then the darkness split open.

A mouth gaped wide where Jacob's head should have been—impossibly large, its jagged teeth shifting, growing, rearranging themselves with sickening cracks. The void inside was endless, swallowing the dim warehouse light, bleeding shadow across the floor. A deep, sucking sound filled the space as the mouth stretched farther, gaping like the maw of something that had spent eternity starving.

Brian screamed.

Aaron barely had time to react before Jacob's hands shot forward, gripping Brian's head with claw-like fingers. Brian thrashed violently, his neck twisting unnaturally under the pressure. His heels scraped against the concrete, his fingers clawing at Aaron's arms, his nails digging deep, but it was useless. Useless.

Jacob inhaled.

The warehouse trembled. The darkness surged forward. Becky felt something twist inside her, like her body was being pulled toward that abyss, her vision blurring at the edges.

Brian's body convulsed violently.

And then—

A sickening, wet pop.

Jacob ripped Brian's head from his body.

Blood gushed in thick, pulsing streams, splattering across the floor in wild arcs. Becky stumbled back, gagging, the raw stench of torn flesh and copper filling her lungs. The body in Aaron's grip twitched, muscles spasming, fingers grasping at nothing, before slumping into dead weight.

But Jacob was not done.

Brian's mouth still moved, a gurgling, wet whisper of words that didn't exist. His lips trembled, his eyelids fluttering, as if some fragment of consciousness remained in that severed head. His eyes locked onto Becky—wide, pleading, horrified.

Jacob pressed the head into the gaping void at his neck.

The shadows folded inward.

Brian's face stretched, distorting as it was pulled into the shifting darkness. His features rippled like something melting, his flesh unraveling, his skull cracking apart. His muffled scream echoed from within Jacob, as though he was still alive—still inside.

The blood that had splattered across the floor lifted.

It moved in unnatural, twisting tendrils, threading through the air like veins seeking their host. The thick rivulets of crimson merged with Jacob, soaking into his body, into his form, his figure becoming more defined, more whole.

Jacob shuddered.

And then he turned to Becky.

His new face—Brian's face—smiled.

The warehouse lights exploded.

The laughter stopped.

Jacob was gone.

The Silence After

Becky and Aaron sat motionless, their bodies trembling. The weight of what they had just done pressed down on them like an unbearable force.

Brian's corpse lay sprawled between them, his lifeless eyes still wide with terror, frozen in the final moments of agony. Blood seeped from the jagged wound in his chest, dark and viscous, pooling onto the cracked concrete like spilled ink. The scent of iron thickened the air, mingling with the damp, musty stench of the abandoned warehouse. A single, flickering fluorescent light buzzed overhead, casting long, erratic shadows that made the scene feel even more surreal.

The air felt... empty.

For the first time in weeks, there was nothing.

No presence. No whispers. No visions.

Jacob was gone.

Becky let out a strangled sob, her fingers clawing at her skin as if she could scrub away the sticky warmth of Brian's blood. It coated her hands, seeped into the creases of her palms, and painted her fingernails in a shade she would never forget. Her chest hitched as she struggled to breathe, her entire body shaking with the force of her grief, her horror.

Aaron sat hunched beside her, his breaths coming hard and fast. He stared at Brian's body like he couldn't quite process what had happened. His knuckles were white where they gripped his knees, and his entire frame was taut as if, at any moment, he might snap under the weight of it all.

The silence was deafening.

And then, the realization hit.

They had murdered a man.

It didn't matter that Brian had been a monster. It didn't matter that it had been necessary. That he would have killed them if given the chance. The fact remained—they had still done it.

And now, there was no going back.

The enormity of their actions hung between them, suffocating, an invisible force pressing down on their lungs. The blood on their hands would never truly wash away, no matter how many times they scrubbed or how many showers they took. It was etched into their souls now, carved into the very fabric of who they were.

Aaron turned to Becky, his voice barely above a whisper, raw and broken.

"It's over."

Becky's breath hitched. She met his gaze, searching for something—reassurance, certainty, absolution—but she found none.

Because she was not sure if she believed him.

CHAPTER TWENTY

The Investigation

The warehouse stood in eerie stillness, the damp air thick with the metallic tang of blood. Blue and red lights painted the cracked pavement outside, their rhythmic flashing reflecting off the rusted metal doors. Inside, officers moved carefully across the stained concrete, their hushed voices barely rising above the hum of forensic equipment.

Detective Matthew Delany adjusted the cuffs of his trench coat, his sharp gaze sweeping over the scene before him. Even after years of working homicide, he had never seen anything quite like this.

A headless corpse lay sprawled in the center of the room, the dark pool beneath it now congealed. No signs of a struggle—no overturned crates, no smeared footprints. Just... this. A body, cleanly decapitated, and not a single damn clue to go with it.

His partner, Detective Rachel Carter, let out a low whistle as she knelt beside the victim, carefully avoiding the thick pool of dried blood. "Jesus," she muttered, pulling on a pair of latex gloves. "No head, no weapon, no prints. You thinking cartel?"

Delany exhaled through his nose. "does not fit. No message. No sign of torture. And the blood splatter's wrong—too clean." He crouched beside her, studying the ragged edges of the neck wound. "This was not done with a blade."

Carter glanced up. "What are you thinking?"

Delany frowned. "Something ripped his head off."

A long silence stretched between them.

"...That's ridiculous," Carter said, standing up and dusting her gloves together. "No defensive wounds, no bruising on the arms, no sign that he was restrained. Either he was already dead before this happened, or—" she exhaled sharply, rubbing her temple. "God, I do not even know."

Delany straightened, turning toward one of the forensic techs. "Anything on the body?"

The tech, a wiry man with thick glasses, shook his head. "No prints, no fibers, no hairs. Whoever did this either knew what they were doing or got ridiculously lucky. We checked the bucket and the rope found near the body—no usable evidence. No purchase records. Nothing."

Delany ran a hand down his face. "So, what you are telling me is we have nothing."

The tech gave a grim nod.

Carter crossed her arms. "Cameras?"

Another officer chimed in from the perimeter. "Negative. No surveillance in or around the building. Nearest camera's about two blocks down, and it's a private system. we areworking on getting access, but chances are whoever did this knew exactly how to avoid being seen."

Delany muttered a curse under his breath.

A professional job—or something so far beyond standard criminal activity that it didn't even make sense.

Carter flipped through her notepad. "Alright, we got an ID on our guy. Brian Foster. No employment records, no parole officer, no family in the area. Guy was a ghost. According to his priors, he had a habit of disappearing for weeks at a time. If we hadn't found the body, who knows how long it would've taken for someone to notice he was missing."

Delany hummed in acknowledgment. "Toxicology?"

"we arerunning it now, but no obvious needle marks. No track lines. Nothing that screams drug-related."

Another dead end.

Delany glanced at the forensic team bagging what little evidence they had. No weapon. No signs of forced entry. No blood trails leading in or out. The more he thought about it, the more unsettling the whole thing became.

Carter leaned in. "You know what this reminds me of?"

Delany raised a brow.

"That car accident case from a few weeks ago. You remember? The one with the kid they found headless?"

Delany stiffened slightly, his jaw tightening. "Yeah. I remember."

"Two headless bodies in less than a month?" Carter shook her head. "Come on, Matt. That's a pattern."

Delany exhaled sharply. "It's a coincidence."

Carter frowned. "Is it?"

Delany didn't answer.

Because the truth was, it didn't feel like a coincidence. Not at all.

And that? That was a problem.

Aftermath of the Investigation

A few hours later, Delany stood outside the warehouse, the cold wind cutting through his coat as he stared at the empty streets. The case was already going cold. No leads. No suspects. No goddamn evidence.

Brian Foster had been erased.

There was something unnatural about the whole thing—like the crime scene itself had been scrubbed clean by forces beyond their understanding.

Carter approached, hands stuffed in her pockets. "What do we put in the report?"

Delany sighed, rubbing his forehead. "We call it what it is—a murder with no leads. We keep digging, see if anything shakes loose."

Carter hesitated. "And if it does not?"

Delany didn't answer right away. Instead, he looked back at the warehouse, at the darkened space where Brian's body had once been.

Then, finally, he spoke.

"Then it goes cold."

And that was the part that bothered him the most.

Because something told him—deep in his gut—that this case was not over. Not by a long shot.

CHAPTER TWENTY-ONE

A New Beginning

Becky woke with a jolt, her stomach twisting violently. For a moment, she was caught between sleep and wakefulness, her mind slow to catch up with the sharp nausea rolling through her body.

Then it hit her.

She barely had time to shove back the covers before she bolted from the bed, her bare feet slapping against the cool floor as she rushed to the bathroom. She dropped to her knees just as the bile surged up her throat.

The retching was violent, her body convulsing as she emptied her stomach into the toilet. Cold sweat beaded along her forehead, her hands gripping the porcelain as she gasped for breath.

Aaron was at her side in seconds.

"Beck—" His voice was thick with sleep and worry as he crouched beside her, his hand rubbing slow circles over her back. "What's wrong? Are you sick?"

Becky shook her head, swallowing past the lump in her throat. "I... I do not know."

She pressed her forehead against the cool porcelain, willing the nausea to pass. But as the seconds stretched on, something else nagged at her—something deeper than the sickness, something pulling at the edges of her memory.

It had been a month since the accident.

A month since the storm. Since Jacob. Since everything had changed.

But it felt like a lifetime.

Her body had been running on adrenaline for so long, she hadn't stopped to notice... hadn't stopped to realize...

Her breath caught in her throat.

The smells.

The coffee Aaron had brewed earlier that morning had made her stomach twist. The scent of his cologne, the same one she had loved for years, had suddenly been too strong. And last night, when he had made her favorite pasta, the garlic had turned her stomach.

She did the math.

The night they had first slept together.

The second time, just days later.

Her heart pounded in her ears.

"Aaron," she whispered, her voice barely audible. She turned to him, her fingers tightening around his wrist. "I... I think I might be pregnant."

Aaron froze.

His eyes locked onto hers, his expression unreadable for a long moment. Then he exhaled, his lips parting in disbelief. "Are you—" He stopped himself, shaking his head. "Are you sure?"

"I do not know." Becky swallowed hard, her voice shaking. "But I need to find out."

Aaron didn't hesitate. He stood, grabbing his keys from the counter. "Let's go."

They didn't speak much on the way to the pharmacy. Becky's hands were clammy in her lap, her stomach twisting—not just from nausea, but from the sheer weight of what this could mean.

She was not ready to think about it yet.

Not until she knew for sure.

Aaron parked in front of the pharmacy, and they walked inside together. The overhead fluorescent lights felt too bright, the air too sterile. Becky hovered in the aisle, staring at the shelves lined with different pregnancy tests, each one a different brand but all promising the same thing.

Aaron grabbed two, just to be sure.

Neither of them spoke as they walked to the register. The cashier barely glanced at them as she rang them up, but Becky swore she could feel the weight of judgment. It was irrational, she knew. People bought pregnancy tests every day.

But it didn't feel normal.

Nothing about this was normal.

A New Chapter

Back at home, Becky paced the bathroom, the unopened boxes sitting on the counter like they held the answer to her entire future.

Aaron leaned against the doorway, watching her. "Do you want me to wait outside?"

She shook her head. "No. Stay."

He nodded, his jaw tightening.

Becky exhaled, steadying herself. Then, with shaky hands, she grabbed one of the tests and disappeared into the bathroom stall.

Minutes passed.

The longest minutes of her life.

She couldn't bring herself to look at the test. Her heart pounded so loudly in her ears she thought she might go deaf.

Then she forced herself to look.

Two pink lines.

Her breath caught. She grabbed the second test. Did it again.

Two pink lines. Again.

Becky pressed a trembling hand over her mouth, her heartbeat hammering against her ribs.

"Oh my God."

Aaron knocked once, his voice gentle. "Beck?"

She opened the door, the test clutched in her hand. She didn't need to say anything.

Aaron's gaze dropped to the test, then back to her face. His breath hitched. "It's—"

Becky nodded, her throat too tight for words.

For a long moment, he just stared at her, something unreadable in his eyes. Then, slowly, the tension in his shoulders eased. His lips parted in awe, and then—

He smiled.

A real, genuine smile.

Becky let out a choked laugh, half a sob, as Aaron reached for her, pulling her into his arms. His grip was strong, grounding, steady—just like he had always been.

"You are pregnant," he whispered against her hair. "We are having a baby."

Becky let out a breath she hadn't realized she'd been holding.

And it felt like everything would be okay for the first time in a long time.

A Promise by the Lake

The lake had become a part of them.

Since the day they found out Becky was pregnant, Aaron had started bringing her here almost every evening. He insisted the walks were good for her, and she couldn't argue with him. The fresh air, the golden hues of autumn, the steady lull of the water—it was a kind of peace she hadn't known in a long time.

A place untouched by the past.

A place that belonged to them.

Today had been no different. Becky thought it was just another visit, another quiet moment in their safe haven. She had spent most of the afternoon leaning against Aaron's side, watching the shifting colors of the sunset paint rippling reflections on the water.

The wind carried the scent of pine and damp earth, wrapping around them in a cool embrace. Leaves crunched beneath their feet as they wandered toward the shore, their steps slow, unhurried.

Becky sighed, rubbing her hands over the sleeves of her sweater. "I used to come here with my parents when I was a kid," she murmured. "I always loved it."

Aaron smiled softly, stuffing his hands into the pockets of his jacket. "I remember you telling me that."

She turned to him then, intending to tease him about his memory. But the words never left her lips.

Because Aaron was looking at her differently.

Like he was memorizing everything about this moment.

It's like he wanted to freeze it in time.

Before she could say anything, he reached into his jacket pocket.

And then—he dropped to one knee.

Becky's breath hitched.

The air shifted around her, the sounds of rustling trees and distant ripples on the water fading into a hush. Everything else—everything that had ever happened, every moment that had brought them to this—fell away.

All that remained was Aaron.

And the small, simple ring he held between his fingers.

No grand speeches. No scripted words. Just him. Looking up at her with quiet certainty, with love, and with the same unwavering steadiness that had kept her standing when the world around them crumbled.

"We made it through hell together," he said, his voice low and thick with emotion. "And I never want to go through anything without you again."

Becky felt something inside her crack, something profound, something she hadn't even realized she had been holding onto.

She thought of everything—the ghosts that had chased them, the blood on their hands, the impossible choices—the weight of survival.

But they had survived.

Aaron had held her through it all. He had never once let go.

And now, here he was, offering her forever.

Not because of what they had done.

But despite it.

Becky's throat tightened. Her vision blurred.

She let out a shaky breath, her lips parting into a trembling smile.

"Yes," she whispered.

Aaron let out a breathless laugh, his shoulders sagging as if he had been holding it in. The relief and happiness on his face were enough to steal whatever air was left in her lungs.

He slid the ring onto her finger—a perfect fit.

Then he was on his feet, and he pulled her into his arms before she could say another word.

Becky buried herself against his chest, inhaling his familiar scent—warmth. She listened to his heartbeat, strong, steady, unshaken.

The past would always be there.

The memories, ghosts, and dark things lurking in the corners of their minds would never fully fade.

But this was real.

This was theirs.

And for the first time in what felt like forever—

She was not haunted.

CHAPTER TWENTY-TWO

A Vow in the Shadows

The wedding was held four years later.

They had wanted to wait.

Not out of fear, hesitation, or the lingering weight of the past—but for Eleanor.

She was old enough now, their bright, shining light, toddling around with the same curiosity that Becky had once carried as a child. They had chosen the name carefully, after endless nights searching through baby girl names, looking for something that felt right. And then they had found it. *Eleanor.*

Greek and Old French.

Bright, shining light.

A symbol of guidance and hope.

She was both. She was everything.

And on this day—their day—she would be their flower girl.

The warm scent of blooming roses and fresh-cut greenery filled the air, blending with the faint salt of the nearby ocean breeze. Soft golden light filtered through the towering oak trees, dappling the aisle with shimmering patches of sunlight. The hush of anticipation settled over the gathered guests as the ceremony began.

And then, Eleanor.

A little giggle bubbled up from the tiny girl as she stepped onto the aisle, her small basket gripped tightly in both hands. Her curls bounced as she moved, and she carefully plucked each petal from the basket before dropping them onto the white runner. Every few steps, she looked up, her wide eyes searching. Then she saw her.

"Mommy!"

A chorus of light chuckles rippled through the guests as Eleanor abandoned all pretenses of gently scattering petals and instead ran toward Becky, her arms outstretched. Becky let out a watery laugh, bending down just in time to catch her daughter, wrapping her up in a tight hug. She smelled like lavender and baby shampoo, the comforting scent grounding Becky in the moment.

"You have to finish your very important job," Becky whispered, brushing a stray curl from Eleanor's face.

Eleanor beamed, nodding solemnly before scampering off to finish her task, her tiny hands tossing petals in every direction as if the whole world should be covered in flowers.

And then, it was Becky's turn.

She took a breath, willing herself to stay composed as the soft melody of the piano filled the air. The moment she stepped forward, the world around her seemed to sharpen—the rustling leaves, the faint hum of the ocean in the distance, the warmth of the sunlight against her skin. Every step felt surreal, like walking through a dream.

Her hands trembled slightly as she clutched the bouquet, not from nerves about the man waiting for her at the altar—but from everything that had brought her here. The weight of the past, once suffocating, now rested lighter on her shoulders.

The insurance check for her car had long since come in, a cold, practical resolution to something that had never truly felt resolved. Instead of replacing the car right away, Becky had used part of it for the wedding. It felt right—taking something born from tragedy and turning it into something beautiful.

She told herself she'd get another car eventually, but even after all this time, she still wasn't ready. The thought of driving alone, of the hum of the tires on a quiet road, still made her stomach twist. The memory of that night had dulled, but it hadn't faded. Not completely.

But she had come so far.

Four years ago, she could barely step outside during a storm without feeling the past clawing at her. Now, she could listen to the rain against the windows without flinching. The shadows that once lurked in her mind had loosened their grip. They would never be completely gone, but they no longer controlled her.

Besides, she had Aaron.

He never minded driving, never made her feel guilty about it. "I like being your personal chauffeur," he always said with a grin. "Makes me feel important."

And today, as he stood at the altar waiting for her, looking at her like she was the only thing in the world—he was.

Just before she reached him, he took a small step forward, as if he physically couldn't wait another second to be near her. His hands reached for hers the moment she was close enough, his fingers warm, grounding.

"You okay?" he murmured, searching her eyes.

Becky nodded, swallowing back the lump in her throat. "Yeah."

Aaron squeezed her hands gently. "You look…" His voice faltered for a moment, emotion thick in his throat before he tried again. "You look breathtaking."

A tear slipped down her cheek before she could stop it, and he caught it with his thumb, brushing it away as he smiled.

And just like that, the weight of the past faded into the background.

Because this moment—this man, their daughter, the life they had built—was all that mattered.

The wedding was held four years later.

They had wanted to wait.

Not out of fear, hesitation, or the lingering weight of the past—but for Eleanor.

She was old enough now, their bright, shining light, toddling around with the same curiosity that Becky had once carried as a child. They had chosen the name carefully, after endless nights searching through baby girl names, looking for something that felt right. And then they had found it. *Eleanor.*

Greek and Old French.

Bright, shining light.

A symbol of guidance and hope.

She was both. She was everything.

And on this day—their day—she would be their flower girl.

The warm scent of blooming roses and fresh-cut greenery filled the air, blending with the faint salt of the nearby ocean breeze. Soft golden light filtered through the towering oak trees, dappling the aisle with shimmering patches of sunlight. The hush of anticipation settled over the gathered guests as the ceremony began.

And then, Eleanor.

A little giggle bubbled up from the tiny girl as she stepped onto the aisle, her small basket gripped tightly in both hands. Her curls bounced as she moved, and she carefully plucked each petal from the basket before dropping them onto the white runner. Every few steps, she looked up, her wide eyes searching. Then she saw her.

"Mommy!"

A chorus of light chuckles rippled through the guests as Eleanor abandoned all pretenses of gently scattering petals and instead ran toward Becky, her arms outstretched. Becky let out a watery laugh, bending down just in time to catch her daughter, wrapping her up in a tight hug. She smelled like lavender and baby shampoo, the comforting scent grounding Becky in the moment.

"You have to finish your very important job," Becky whispered, brushing a stray curl from Eleanor's face.

Eleanor beamed, nodding solemnly before scampering off to finish her task, her tiny hands tossing petals in every direction as if the whole world should be covered in flowers.

And then, it was Becky's turn.

She took a breath, willing herself to stay composed as the soft melody of the piano filled the air. The moment she stepped forward, the world around her seemed to sharpen—the rustling leaves, the faint hum of the ocean in the distance, the warmth of the sunlight against her skin. Every step felt surreal, like walking through a dream.

Her hands trembled slightly as she clutched the bouquet, not from nerves about the man waiting for her at the altar—but from everything that had brought her here. The weight of the past, once suffocating, now rested lighter on her shoulders.

The insurance check for her car had long since come in, a cold, practical resolution to something that had never truly felt resolved. Instead of replacing the car right away, Becky had used part of it for the wedding. It felt right—taking something born from tragedy and turning it into something beautiful.

She told herself she'd get another car eventually, but even after all this time, she still wasn't ready. The thought of driving alone, of the hum of the tires on a quiet road, still made her stomach twist. The memory of that night had dulled, but it hadn't faded. Not completely.

But she had come so far.

Four years ago, she could barely step outside during a storm without feeling the past clawing at her. Now, she could listen to the rain against the windows without flinching. The shadows that once lurked in her mind had loosened their grip. They would never be completely gone, but they no longer controlled her.

Besides, she had Aaron.

He never minded driving, never made her feel guilty about it. "I like being your personal chauffeur," he always said with a grin. "Makes me feel important."

And today, as he stood at the altar waiting for her, looking at her like she was the only thing in the world—he was.

Just before she reached him, he took a small step forward, as if he physically couldn't wait another second to be near her. His hands reached for hers the moment she was close enough, his fingers warm, grounding.

"You okay?" he murmured, searching her eyes.

Becky nodded, swallowing back the lump in her throat. "Yeah."

Aaron squeezed her hands gently. "You look..." His voice faltered for a moment, emotion thick in his throat before he tried again. "You look breathtaking."

A tear slipped down her cheek before she could stop it, and he caught it with his thumb, brushing it away as he smiled.

And just like that, the weight of the past faded into the background.

Because this moment—this man, their daughter, the life they had built—was all that mattered.

Ever After

Aaron stood at the altar, his hands clasped before him, his pulse a steady, thundering drumbeat in his ears. He was not nervous—not in the way most grooms were. He had no doubts, no cold feet.

He had waited four years for this.

For her.

For forever.

Rows of chairs lined the open-air venue, the golden afternoon sunlight filtering through the towering trees and casting shadows across the gathered guests. Everyone was there—friends, family, and people who had no idea what he and Becky had endured to get here.

They smiled, they whispered, and they waited.

A photographer moved through the crowd, capturing everything—the soft hum of conversation, the gentle rustle of autumn leaves, the tiny flower girl giggling as she tossed petals along the aisle.

Eleanor.

She was a vision in white, her tiny fingers clutching the basket with serious concentration, her curls bouncing with every step. The guests adored her. Some laughed softly; some wiped away sentimental tears.

Aaron's heart clenched.

His daughter.

His whole world.

Then, the music changed.

Every head turned.

And there she was.

Becky stepped into view, her arm gently linked with her father's.

Aaron swore the earth stopped turning.

She was radiant.

The dress flowed around her, lace brushing the ground like mist over water. The sunset caught in her curls, turning them into liquid gold. But it was not the dress or the way the fabric hugged her curves, or the sunlight adored her—it was how she smiled.

It was real.

Not borrowed, not forced.

Not shadowed by the past.

Aaron exhaled, tension easing from his shoulders.

The last four years had been good to them.

The memories still lingered, but their weight had lessened. The nightmares had become rare, and the visions had faded.

It was over.

They had won.

Becky walked toward him, and nothing else existed.

Not the guests.

Not the whispering breeze.

Not the world beyond this moment.

Just her.

And then—

A chill ran down Aaron's spine.

Subtle at first.

Like the faint brush of ice against his skin.

His gaze flicked beyond Becky, beyond the guests, beyond the moment.

And there he was.

Still. Silent. Watching.

A gray hoodie.

Bloodstained.

No head.

Aaron's breath caught.

His chest constricted, the world tilting—No. No, this isn't real.

His mind screamed at him, begging him to look away, to pretend he hadn't seen.

But he felt it.

The same oppressive weight.

The same presence that had haunted them, tormented them.

Jacob Hayes.

The thing they had killed for.

The thing they had sacrificed to be free from.

No.

No, he was gone.

They had won.

Or had they?

Aaron's hands curled into fists. His body tensed, his pulse pounding in his throat.

And then—his eyes darted to Becky.

She was holding Eleanor.

Oblivious.

She was smiling.

Untouched by the terror gripping his chest.

Aaron thanked God for that.

Because no matter what this was—his mind, a ghost, a trick of the light—Becky didn't see him.

No one else reacted.

Maybe... maybe it was in his head.

Aaron blinked.

The man was gone.

Just like that.

Like he had never been there at all.

But Aaron knew what he had seen.

And deep down, in the darkest corner of himself, he knew what it meant.

Sealed With a Kiss

Becky finally reached the altar, her steps slow and deliberate, the golden light of the setting sun painting everything in a soft glow. The world felt like it was holding its breath.

Aaron barely breathed.

His eyes locked onto hers, searching, holding onto this moment—this reality. The lingering chill of his earlier vision still clung to him, but Becky's presence, her warmth, her steady hand in his, was enough to keep him grounded.

This was their day.

This was real.

She was real.

Becky's fingers slipped into his—warm, steady, grounding. Aaron exhaled, his grip tightening around hers. For a second, just a second, his gaze flicked past her shoulder. Searching.

Nothing.

Only the guests. The sun filtering through the trees. The whisper of the wind. The soft rustling of Eleanor's flower petals against the grass.

Maybe he had imagined it.

Maybe his mind was still trapped in the past.

Aaron swallowed hard, forcing his attention back to Becky.

She was looking at him, her brows knitting together slightly.

"Aaron?" Her voice was gentle, searching. "Are you okay?"

He hesitated—a heartbeat too long.

Then, he forced a smile.

"Yeah," he whispered. "I'm okay."

Becky held his gaze for a second longer, as if trying to read the truth in his expression.

Then, she smiled.

And just like that, the fear faded.

The officiant cleared his throat.

"Dearly beloved, we are gathered here today..."

The words blurred, a distant hum beneath Aaron's pulse.

He barely heard a thing.

His mind was still tangled in what he had seen.

Had it been in his mind? A trick of the light? A shadow playing cruel tricks on him?

Or was it something worse?

Aaron clenched Becky's fingers just a little tighter.

Then—Becky's voice cut through the fog.

Soft. Steady.

Filled with love.

Aaron blinked, anchoring himself back to the moment.

Becky was saying her vows, her voice firm, unwavering.

There was no hesitation in her words. No shadows clinging to her.

Just love.

Love that had been tested in ways no love should ever be tested.

Love that had survived.

And Aaron—hearing it, feeling it—let the past slip away.

For now.

The officiant turned to him.

Aaron's breath caught—his turn.

He met Becky's eyes, and his voice found him.

His throat was dry, but the words came quickly.

Because they weren't just words.

They were a promise.

A vow that, no matter what came next, he would never let her go.

"I do."

He slid the ring onto Becky's finger, his touch steady, reverent.

The moment stretched—golden, endless.

"You may kiss the bride," the officiant announced.

Aaron didn't hesitate.

He pulled her close, his lips capturing hers as the guests erupted into cheers.

For a moment—just a moment—the world was bright and full.

Laughter. Applause. The warmth of Becky's hands in his.

They had survived.

They had won.

And then—

A tiny giggle.

Aaron pulled back just enough to glance down, his heart swelling at the sight of their daughter standing beside them, her little hands clasped together in excitement.

Eleanor.

She had been perfect today—her tiny white dress fluttering with every step as she had scattered flower petals down the aisle, her curls bouncing, her face lit with an innocent joy that made Aaron believe—just for a moment—that maybe, just maybe, everything was truly okay.

She looked up at him now, wide-eyed and delighted.

Aaron grinned and swooped her into his arms, lifting her high.

Eleanor squealed with laughter, wrapping her tiny arms around his neck.

Becky leaned in, pressing a soft kiss to Eleanor's cheek. Aaron followed, planting one of his own on the other side.

Eleanor wriggled in his hold, giggling.

The crowd melted.

Laughter. Awe. More cheers.

This moment was theirs.

A family.

Whole.

Complete.

Aaron felt it then—something deep, something unshakable settling in his chest.

They had been through hell.

But this—this was heaven.

And nothing—nothing—was ever going to take it away.

Not the past.

Not the ghosts.

Not even Jacob Hayes.

Aaron exhaled, squeezing Becky's hand as he looked at her.

"We did it," she whispered, her voice filled with emotion.

Aaron kissed her again, held her close, held Eleanor even closer.

And forced himself to believe it.

Because it was their wedding day.

Because they deserved this moment.

Because if the past was not done with them—

He was not ready to know.

Afterword

Some stories never truly leave you. They linger in your mind, waiting for the right moment to be told. *Echoes of the Rain* is one of those stories.

For years, this story lived in my head and collected dust in a forgotten folder on my computer. It went through changes, rewrites, and complete overhauls—always evolving, but never quite finished. It was originally titled *The Accident*, a name that felt too blunt, too direct. The heart of the story wasn't just about an accident; it was about memories, lingering echoes of the past, and the way certain moments can haunt us long after they're over. *Echoes of the Rain* felt more fitting. It carried the weight of Becky's past, the storm that shaped her fate, and the presence of something—or someone—she could never truly escape.

This book took me longer to finish than I ever expected. There were moments when I doubted it would ever be completed, times when I convinced myself it wasn't good enough or that it simply wasn't meant to be. I would open the file, tweak a few lines, rework a scene, and then abandon it again. But no matter how many times I set it aside, it always pulled me back.

In a way, I see a lot of myself in Becky. Like her, I was born during a massive storm. The power had gone out at the hospital, and lightning actually struck my grandmother's house that same day. Maybe it was fate, but I've always been drawn to storms. I find them relaxing—the rolling thunder, the rhythm of rain against the windows, and that distinct earthy smell that lingers in the air afterward. (*Petrichor*, as I later learned it's called.) I may not be as obsessed with them as Becky, but I understand her fascination.

For a long time, *Echoes of the Rain* remained unfinished, just another lingering echo in my mind. Then, something changed. I found my way back to writing through short stories—stories I had once written for fun, tucked away and forgotten. I started expanding them, shaping them into something more, and that journey led to my first published book, *Fragments of Fear: Seven Tales of Darkness and Dread*. Completing that collection rekindled my love for storytelling, and it reminded me why I started writing in the first place.

Once *Fragments of Fear* was finished, I knew I had unfinished business. *Echoes of the Rain* had waited long enough. It was time to complete the story, to give these characters the ending they deserved. And now, here it is—the book that haunted me for years, finally brought to life.

But this is only the beginning.

Another story still lingers—one that has been abandoned even longer than *Echoes of the Rain*. *The Letter*, is what I originally titled it; I am still working on it along with other projects. I am making a promise to myself to finish *The Letter* before I turn 40, I am currently 38 as I write this. I know I can do it.

My next project, *The Last Run*, has consumed my thoughts in the same way this book once did. It follows Olivia Carter, a seventeen-year-old track star who longs to escape her small town, only to fall into the hands of someone far more dangerous than she ever imagined. It is a story of desperation, survival, and the consequences of being forgotten. Much like *Echoes of the Rain*, this story refuses to be ignored, and I am ready to bring it to life.

Before I close, I want to take a moment to thank my friends who pushed me to finish my long-overdue projects. Without that encouragement, this book might still be sitting unfinished in the depths of my hard drive. And to the readers—thank you for taking this journey with me. I hope *Echoes of the Rain* lingers with you the way it always lingers with me.

— R. Rivera

About the author

R. Rivera is a passionate storyteller who thrives on crafting immersive, suspenseful tales that pull readers in from the very first page. Born in Houston, Texas, in 1987, he has called the small town of Uvalde home since 1994. His love for writing emerged early, particularly during school State Tests, where he eagerly embraced the writing prompts that others dreaded—often writing far beyond the required word count.

Rivera's passion for storytelling was ignited in childhood by reading the Goosebumps *series in its entirety and Scary Stories to Tell in the Dark. As* he grew older, he found inspiration in authors like Stephen King, Joe Hill, and Anne Rice. Reading *The Shining* at just 12 years old left a lasting impression, sparking a fascination with suspense and psychological horror that continues to shape his writing today. He enjoys adding unexpected twists to his stories, making each one an unforgettable experience. While thrillers and suspense dominate his work, he occasionally ventures into other genres, always seeking new ways to challenge and engage his readers.

Balancing two jobs alongside his writing isn't easy, but Rivera dedicates his weekends to bringing his stories to life. During the week, he's constantly jotting down ideas in a notebook or on his phone, ensuring inspiration is never lost. When he's not writing, he enjoys gaming, solving puzzles, and traveling—especially on his yearly cruise.

His ultimate goal is to create characters and narratives that resonate deeply, evoking raw emotions in his audience. If his writing can make someone cry, laugh, or feel truly connected to his characters, then he knows he has succeeded. Readers can explore his chilling collection, *Fragments of Fear*, and look forward to his upcoming projects. With each new story, R. Rivera invites readers on a thrilling journey into the unknown—where fear and fascination intertwine.

www.ingramcontent.com/pod-product-compliance
Lightning Source LLC
Chambersburg PA
CBHW051059030726
47504CB00006B/1698